SECRETS OF BEARHAVEN

BOOK THREE

HIDDEN ROCK RESCUE

Don't miss all the exciting adventures!

Secrets of Bearhaven Book 1

Secrets of Bearhaven Book 2:
Mission to Moon Farm

SECRETS OF BEARHAVEN

BOOK THREE

HIDDEN ROCK RESCUE

K. E. ROCHA

SCHOLASTIC PRESS / NEW YORK

All rights reserved. Published by Scholastic Press, an imprint of Scholastic Inc., *Publishers since 1920*. SCHOLASTIC, SCHOLASTIC PRESS, and associated logos are trademarks and/or registered trademarks of Scholastic Inc.

The publisher does not have any control over and does not assume any responsibility for author or third-party websites or their content.

No part of this publication may be reproduced, stored in a retrieval system, or transmitted in any form or by any means, electronic, mechanical, photocopying, recording, or otherwise, without written permission of the publisher. For information regarding permission, write to Scholastic Inc., Attention: Permissions Department, 557 Broadway, New York, NY 10012.

This book is a work of fiction. Names, characters, places, and incidents are either the product of the author's imagination or are used fictitiously, and any resemblance to actual persons, living or dead, business establishments, events, or locales is entirely coincidental.

Library of Congress Cataloging-in-Publication Data available

ISBN 978-0-545-81305-1

10 9 8 7 6 5 4 3 2 1   17 18 19 20 21

Printed in the U.S.A.   23

First edition, January 2017
Book design by Nina Goffi

For Will Russell, for being my Aldo in every adventure

SECRETS OF
BEARHAVEN

BOOK THREE

HIDDEN ROCK
RESCUE

1

Spencer Plain threw rocks and twigs aside frantically as he searched the ground for his jade bear. He rushed forward, following the row of bushes he'd hidden behind last night. *It has to be here!*

He tore his eyes away from the dirt to glance up at the sky. It was almost midmorning. He was running out of time.

He jumped to his feet and headed for one of the trees he was sure he'd climbed. He did a lap around the huge tree trunk, his eyes glued to the ground, then turned around to do another lap in the opposite direction and bumped straight into Kate Weaver.

"Oof!" He stumbled backward, startled.

"Oops!" exclaimed Kate, the chestnut-colored cub who was just scrambling down from the tree branches. "I didn't see you."

"Did you find it?" Spencer asked. He glanced at the glimmering device around Kate's neck, the BEAR-COM that translated the bears' language, Ragayo, into English. He willed it to translate the Ragayo word for "yes." It didn't.

"Not yet," Kate replied. She hurried to a nearby tree.

Her bandaged ear bobbed as she ran. She started sniffing the ground.

"It could be anywhere!" Spencer didn't mean to yell, but today, of all the days in his whole life, was the worst possible one to lose his jade bear.

"Not *anywhere*," Kate said. "It fell out of your pocket during training last night, right?"

"Right," Spencer agreed.

"Well, this is where we trained, so it has to be here somewhere!"

Spencer nodded. Last night after dinner, he and Kate had come here, to the Bear Stealth training field in Bearhaven's school yard, to practice some of Spencer's operative skills. He was leaving on a rescue mission today, and he had wanted to make sure he was really ready. He had run and climbed and tumbled and crawled and done a million other spy-like moves. And at the end of it all, when he got back to the Weavers' house, where he was staying, he felt really ready. Until he discovered that at some point in all that training, the jade bear had slipped out of his pocket.

So Spencer was retracing his steps around the Bear Stealth training field at a sprint, searching for the small black jade figurine he *always* kept in his pocket. Mom and Dad had given it to him on his eighth birthday. It made him feel stronger, braver, and closer to them, and he had never gone on a rescue mission without it. Today was definitely *not* the day to start because today he wasn't leaving on just any rescue. He was leaving on the most important mission of all: to save his parents.

Something shiny and black caught Spencer's eye. He dove

for it, snatching up a whole handful of earth as he grabbed for the jade bear. He opened his fingers and brushed dirt away from the shiny black object in his palm. Just a rock. Spencer threw it to the ground angrily. Kate was watching him. He shook his head.

"We'll find it," Kate said, resuming her hunt.

"We have to," Spencer muttered, thankful, at least, that he wasn't searching alone. Kate was Spencer's best friend in Bearhaven. He couldn't imagine what he would do without her. Only a week ago, Spencer had made a mistake that landed Kate in terrible danger, and there had been a chance he would never see Kate again.

Luckily, Spencer and a Bearhaven rescue team had saved Kate and brought her home three days ago. But the bandage on her ear where she had been painfully pierced with a metal tag was a reminder that seriously evil criminals had almost taken Kate away from her family and Spencer—and Bearhaven—forever. Those people—Pam, Margo, and Ivan—were the very same ones who were holding Mom and Dad prisoner now.

Pam was a bear-obsessed creep who was behind numerous terrible and illegal things that were happening to bears. His employees, Margo and Ivan Lalicki, a sister-and-brother team who did Pam's dirty work, were almost as dangerous and definitely as creepy.

"What if I don't find it, Kate?" Spencer said, his voice catching in his throat as he started to panic. He had faced Pam, Margo, and Ivan before but never without the jade bear in his pocket. What if without it, Spencer wasn't brave enough to save Mom and Dad? What if the jade bear really did have the power to make him stronger? "We're probably late already."

Just then, as though on cue, a black-and-brown bear came running around the side of the school building shouting their names.

"Kate! Spencer!" It was Aldo Weaver, Kate's older brother. *No!* Spencer's stomach twisted. They were out of time.

"What am I going to do?!" he whispered.

Kate shot him a wide-eyed look.

"It's time to go," Aldo called.

"Spencer's not ready yet!" Kate piped up. Spencer dropped his eyes to the ground and kicked the shiny black rock. He hated the idea of leaving on the mission without his jade bear, but Spencer didn't want to admit to Aldo *why* he wasn't ready. He didn't want to sound like a baby.

Aldo looked from Kate to Spencer. The silver cuffs on his two front legs that marked him as a member of the Bear Guard, Bearhaven's security force, reflected the sunshine.

"We have to go," Aldo said. Even though Aldo was on the guard, he was almost as new to being a Bearhaven operative as Spencer was, and he and Spencer *both* knew it wouldn't look good if the two newest operatives were late for the mission send-off.

Spencer gulped. "Yeah," he said, nodding. "I guess we'd better hurry."

"Come on!" Aldo turned and led the way around the side of the school building at a run.

Kate hesitated. "What about your jade bear?" she whispered.

"I guess I have to leave without it." He tried to sound

4

confident as he broke into a jog. Kate fell in beside him, and together they took off after Aldo.

As he ran, Spencer tried to shake the feeling that Mom and Dad's rescue was already off to a bad start. And he and the rest of the operatives hadn't even made it out of Bearhaven yet.

2

Spencer and Kate raced through the outskirts of Bearhaven after Aldo, who had picked up speed. When the larger bear started up a hill, Spencer looked beyond him, to the hilltop where a row of figures stood, shadowed by trees, overlooking Bearhaven's hidden valley. He started to run faster.

"There you are, Spence!" a voice called from the tree line. It was Spencer's uncle Mark, the only other human in Bearhaven right now. Spencer and Kate reached the top of the hill a good minute after Aldo.

Uh-oh. They were late. Everyone else was already here. Kate bounded over to her parents, Professor Weaver and Bunny Weaver, who were standing with the rest of the Bear Council.

B.D., the Head of the Bear Guard and the largest, strongest bear in Bearhaven, shot Spencer a reprimanding look. Just like Aldo, B.D. wore the guard's silver cuffs on his two front legs.

"I would've thought you'd be here at the crack of dawn," Uncle Mark commented, waving Spencer over. "You've been waiting for this day since your parents went missing."

"Sorry, I was just . . . doing some last-minute training."

Spencer went to stand with the other operatives. There was Uncle Mark, who looked as cool and collected as ever in a leather jacket and black jeans; Aldo, who was trying hard to hide his eagerness to set off on a new rescue mission; and B.D., who rose up onto his massive hind legs, taking charge.

"All right, that's everyone," B.D. announced, looking down the row of bears and humans who had gathered for the mission send-off. Spencer followed B.D.'s gaze. The eight other bear members of the council stood to one side of B.D. They were the bears who made the most important decisions for Bearhaven. B.D. was on the council, and so were Uncle Mark, Mom, and Dad because they had helped to create Bearhaven. Just thinking about how Mom and Dad had been part of the team that built this secret, safe haven for bears still made Spencer swell with pride. He had only learned about Bearhaven's existence three weeks ago, when his parents first disappeared, and since then, Spencer had discovered that Mom and Dad had rescued almost all the bears who lived here.

B.D. continued, "Today Mark, Aldo, Spencer, and I will be departing on a mission of the utmost importance to the Bearhaven community. In our absence, the remaining members of Bearhaven's council will oversee the continuing preparations . . ."

Spencer saw B.D. hesitate, and goose bumps rose on his arms. B.D. *never* hesitated.

The bear looked away from the council and down into the valley of Bearhaven. Spencer followed his gaze. In the distance, Spencer spotted the glint of the special metal that encased the dome-shaped Lab. A wide river curled around the outskirts of the valley, and a path led from the dock beside the river into Bearhaven's center. It passed the schoolhouse and the Bear Guard's training grounds before reaching the middle of the valley, where a tall flagpole stood. Bears following their daily routines moved along the paths that arched around rows of moss-covered homes. They looked so safe in the morning sun . . .

Spencer guessed B.D. had stopped short of talking about "the continuing preparations" because he didn't want to scare Kate by mentioning the danger facing Bearhaven now. And what it was exactly that Bearhaven was continuing to prepare for.

Professor Weaver spoke up. "Everything here will continue as planned," he said, signaling to B.D. and the rest of the group that B.D.'s message—get ready to protect Bearhaven—had been understood.

"Speaking of preparations . . ." Chef Raymond reached out a claw and tapped a box on the ground beside him, startling Kate, who had been sniffing curiously at its edges. "B.D., there's a fresh batch of homemade Raymond's fuel bars in here for the mission."

"Thank you." B.D. nodded at Raymond, finally taking his eyes off the flagpole at the center of Bearhaven, where two flags snapped back and forth in the wind.

"Well," said Grandmama Grizabelle, the oldest bear on the council. "Nobody's going to get rescued if we all just stand here chitchatting," she said frankly. "Good luck, gentlemen." She looked from Spencer, to Uncle Mark, to Aldo, and back to B.D. "I hope the next time we're all here together it will be to welcome more of the Bearhaven family home."

"And don't forget!" Kate suddenly exclaimed. Bunny Weaver tried to quiet her, but the cub ignored her mother. "My concert is in nine days. And I. Have. Been. Practicing. So you have to be home by then." She looked at Spencer and Aldo, waiting for them to promise they would be.

Spencer smiled. Kate was not quite as happy and playful as she had been before she was kidnapped by Margo and Ivan Lalicki and kept as a prisoner by Pam on his evil Moon Farm island. But even though she was not 100 percent back to her old self, one thing hadn't changed. She was still incredibly excited to perform her first solo in her family's band, the Weaver Family Singers, and she expected *everyone* to be at the concert to see her perform. No excuses.

"We'll be here, Kate," Aldo promised.

"Well, now *that's* settled." Uncle Mark chuckled. "How about we get *this* show on the road?"

They all looked to B.D. The bear nodded solemnly. Spencer knew how important this mission was, not just for him and his family, but for B.D., and all of Bearhaven.

B.D. stepped out to face the group. He lifted a claw to his BEAR-COM and switched it off so that his Ragayo would come out untranslated. Spencer remembered this was exactly what B.D. had done before the team left Bearhaven last week to rescue Kate. *"Abragan,"* B.D. growled.

"For the bears," everyone on the hilltop replied. And with that, the rescue team had officially been sent off.

3

Spencer stood beside a medium-sized white plane with copper-tinted windows. Its sleek exterior reminded him at once of the TUBE, Bearhaven's train, and now Spencer knew why it looked familiar. Uncle Mark had just told him that this special plane was also part of Bearhaven's transportation fleet. Spencer kept staring at it in awe, just like he had been doing for the past five minutes, imagining Mom and Dad jetting off on rescue missions all over the country. He could hardly believe he was about to do the very same thing.

"Hey, you!" Evarita emerged from the plane. "Don't you want to see the inside?"

Evarita was Mom and Dad's assistant, and back home, she stayed with Spencer when Mom and Dad traveled. Since his parents' disappearance, Spencer had learned Evarita was *also* a backup operative for Bearhaven, proving she was even cooler than he'd ever suspected. She usually did the research that helped Bearhaven's team plan its missions, and today she was handling transportation.

"Yeah!" Spencer cheered, eager to see if the plane's interior had as much state-of-the-art technology as the TUBE.

"Well, come on, then." Evarita disappeared back under

the canopy covering the stairs. Spencer rushed to follow her onto the plane.

"Evarita, does Bearhaven have a pilot?" Spencer asked, wondering what kind of pilot would be available to fly bears all over the country.

"Yeah, of course." Evarita laughed. "Me."

"No way!"

"Don't sound so surprised!" Evarita headed for the cockpit. She made her way through the passenger area, where four comfortable-looking seats faced two huge video screens. On the other side of the plane were a few big, sturdy seats that looked like they'd been specially made for bear operatives. Aldo and B.D. had already settled themselves there.

"Spencer, watch this," Aldo called. He reached out a claw and touched something on the wall beside him. All of a sudden, a copper-colored panel came down from the roof above Aldo's head. It slid down in front of the space where Aldo sat. When it reached the floor, it clicked into place, completely hiding Aldo from view. Spencer walked over and knocked on the shell. It looked like a piece of the plane, like a cargo section of the cabin or a specially designed wall.

"That could come in handy!" Spencer shouted.

"It's not soundproof," B.D. grumbled. "He can hear you." Spencer looked over his shoulder at B.D. The bigger bear had the same button and folded-up copper shell above his head as Aldo. In an emergency, they'd be able to hide both bears completely, even on this small plane.

Whoosh.

Spencer turned back to Aldo. The shell was rising, folding back into place above Aldo's head.

"That was awesome," Spencer whispered to Aldo, then continued into the rear section of the plane, which held what Spencer guessed was a collection of operative gear. There were no windows in the back. Instead, shiny white drawers were stacked one on top of another, lining the wall and arching toward the center, following the curve of the plane.

"So what do you think, Spence?" Uncle Mark stepped into the cabin. He strode over to where Spencer stood reaching for a drawer labeled "rope."

"It's like a compact version of the TUBE," Spencer answered. He opened the drawer. Six coils of rope lay neatly inside. Each rope was a different width or texture. "Actually, this plane might be even *cooler* than the TUBE."

Uncle Mark laughed. "There are tools here," he said, pointing to a section of drawers. "Medical supplies here." He pointed to another five or six drawers. "Night-vision goggles are in here. Ear-COMs are over there, and handheld walkie-talkies are there." Uncle Mark continued to point out different drawers. He showed Spencer where Raymond's fuel bars were and where the prosthetics were for the more serious disguises. He even pointed out a drawer filled with recording devices like cameras and audio recorders. "You have your backpack with you?"

"Yeah, right here," Spencer answered. He slipped the black backpack off his back as Uncle Mark retrieved a crumpled piece of paper from his pocket. He handed the paper to Spencer.

"Why don't you fill your own mission pack this time? Here's a list of things you must have, but you can add whatever else you think you might need. Just don't make your pack too heavy—that's a rookie mistake—and don't forget rope."

Spencer's excitement spiked. He could take *any* of this operative gear with him!

"I'm going to see what else needs to be done before we take off," Uncle Mark said, heading toward the cockpit. "Call me if you don't know what something is."

Spencer didn't answer. He was already focused on checking Uncle Mark's list and filling his backpack with supplies for the mission ahead.

4

Just as Spencer was dropping a slingshot into his backpack, Evarita's voice rang out of the cockpit. "Time to find your seats and prepare for takeoff."

Spencer slung his backpack over one shoulder and headed up to the passenger area of the small plane. He dropped into the seat beside Uncle Mark and fastened his seat belt, then turned to check on Aldo and B.D. The bears sat back on their haunches. A strap crossed each of their chests and was fastened to the wall of the plane behind them—bear-sized seat belts. A screen was lowering down between B.D. and Aldo, so anything that played on the video screens in front of Spencer and Uncle Mark would be shown to the bear operatives, too.

"Once we're up in the air, we'll do a full brief on the mission ahead." Evarita's voice carried into the cabin through speakers over Spencer's head. He watched as three images popped up on the screen in front of him.

The plane started moving, picking up speed. Evarita propelled them smoothly into the air, but Spencer hardly noticed. He was too focused on the screen in front of him, where pictures of Mom and Dad were displayed and, beside them, a picture of a jet-black bear. The bear was Dora, B.D.'s long-lost sister.

"All right, we've reached our cruising altitude. Let's get started," Evarita said.

"Certainly," B.D. said. "To review, we have to make three rescues tonight: Jane and Shane Plain, and . . ." Spencer didn't dare look back at B.D. He knew the next name B.D. said would be the bear's own sister's, and that her rescue was more important to B.D. than anything. "Dora Benally," B.D. said after a moment, adding his and Dora's last name to make the brief sound as official as possible. "Jane and Shane are currently being held captive by Pam," B.D. hurried on. "We believe Pam is trying to use them to gain access to Bearhaven."

Spencer nodded. *This* was what B.D. hadn't wanted to say in front of Kate. He didn't want to scare her with the news that Pam was going to attack Bearhaven. Pam had been training an army of eighty-eight bears, preparing them to attack Bearhaven as soon as he discovered its location. He believed Jane and Shane would lead him to the bears' secret community so he could invade and capture the bears of Bearhaven.

"Dora is a different story," B.D. continued. Spencer examined the picture of Dora. "This photo was taken twelve years ago, when we—Dora, John Shirley, and I—were still mascots at Gutler University. As we are all well aware, Dora was meant to be rescued in that first-ever mission, but . . . she was not."

Spencer knew it had haunted B.D. for twelve years that only he and his brother, John Shirley, had been rescued from

Gutler University but that Dora hadn't been. Mom, Dad, and Uncle Mark had not been able to get her out. They had returned later for Dora, but all they found was a scrap of the jersey she'd been made to wear as a mascot. That green-and-gold scrap of fabric had flown as one of the flags in Bearhaven ever since, but Dora had never been seen again. That is, until last week, when Spencer had seen her himself.

"While we were all at Moon Farm, working to rescue Kate and locate Jane and Shane, two important discoveries were made," B.D. said as the screen changed. Now, black-and-white video footage played across it. The scene in the video was familiar, though seeing Moon Farm, Pam's illegal bear-smuggling facility, still made Spencer cringe. The video was of Pam and Dora, side by side, overlooking the eighty-eight-bear army in the middle of the night. "Dora belongs to Pam now. He keeps her with him—separate from the bears he sells or uses in the army." B.D. sounded disgusted by the idea of Dora belonging to Pam.

"We believe Dora is more of a companion animal than a captive," Uncle Mark jumped in. "I was also able to locate Pam's home, where Jane and Shane are being held, and where we can expect Dora to be tonight." The screen changed again, this time to a map with a blazing red dot in Nevada.

"Finally," B.D. said, taking over the brief again, "there's a reason we've planned this mission for tonight. Evarita discovered that Pam is hosting an event at his home this evening. This party, whatever it's for, should provide us the cover we need to make our rescues."

"I've made another discovery you all should know about," Evarita chimed in from the cockpit. "Since Mark turned over the location of Pam's estate to me, I've been working to uncover anything I can about it. Have you all heard of Hidden Rock Zoo?"

"No," Spencer answered right away.

"Hidden Rock Zoo is a legendary zoo in Nevada. It had the largest collection of bears of any zoo in the country, and a state-of-the-art design," Uncle Mark explained. "A month after opening, a private owner paid some insane amount of money to buy it. The buyer closed the zoo to the public permanently."

"The zoo has been a complete mystery ever since," Evarita said. "It's on the outskirts of a town in Nevada, but nobody bothers to even go near it anymore. There's no point. The security is impossible, and huge walls were built to block any views inside."

"Let me guess," B.D. growled. "Pam was the mystery buyer."

"Exactly," Evarita said. "The location of Pam's home is identical to the location of Hidden Rock Zoo."

"You mean . . ." Spencer started, trying to understand. "Pam lives in a zoo? Mom and Dad are locked up . . . in a zoo?" *Creepy.*

"Yes. Well, Pam lives in what *was* a zoo." Evarita's voice filled the small plane's cabin. "The year after Pam bought Hidden Rock Zoo, millions of dollars were spent on renovations, but the company that did the work was sworn to secrecy. They could never reveal even a single detail about the work they did on the property."

"So it could look like anything now," B.D. said, his voice grim.

As though to fight the sudden darkening of the mood in the plane, a colorful, cartoonish map appeared on the video screens. *Hidden Rock Zoo!* was printed in bright red letters at the top of the map.

"All we have to go on is an old zoo map," Evarita said. "But it's better than nothing."

5

Spencer handed Uncle Mark a nose. They were in the back of Bearhaven's plane on the ground at a private airport twenty minutes from Hidden Rock Zoo, and Uncle Mark was halfway through disguising his face with prosthetics. Spencer couldn't take his eyes off Uncle Mark gluing a fake forehead over his own natural one, changing the whole shape of his face. Once he added the prosthetic nose, Spencer knew his uncle would look like a total stranger. Spencer was happy to watch Uncle Mark completing his disguise: The prosthetics were a good distraction from the rising tension on Bearhaven's plane.

"All right, I'm finally getting somewhere," Evarita broke the silence. She was sitting cross-legged in one of the swiveling passenger chairs. Her laptop was open on her lap, and papers were spread out on the floor of the plane around her.

"Have you ID'd any of them?" B.D. asked from his place beneath the scrolling copper shell. Neither he nor Aldo had moved from their seats since takeoff. Once Evarita landed Bearhaven's plane, they'd discovered that even getting within a hundred miles of Hidden Rock Zoo was way more dangerous than expected.

Spencer looked away from Uncle Mark's changing face to peek out one of the windows again. The private airport was packed with planes, all of them much creepier, and more sinister-looking, than Bearhaven's plane. The one parked right beside them was all black, except for the tail and the tips of the wings, which were bloodred. Another plane was white with a logo painted in gray on the body. The logo faded into the white of the plane, like it wasn't really meant to be seen. It showed a single bear paw. Spencer didn't know why, but the ghostlike bear paw gave him a very bad feeling. Almost as bad a feeling as the name printed on another plane in the row. *Hook, Line, and Skinner* it read. *That* plane had tipped Evarita off. There was something very wrong about the kinds of planes crowding the private airport.

"Yes," Evarita answered B.D. "And it's exactly what I was afraid of. *Hook, Line, and Skinner* belongs to Lucian Line, a known international animal dealer. And the plane with the red on it is Vera Degarmo's. She's another black-market dealer."

"What about the one with the gray bear paw?" Spencer asked.

"I can't ID that one, but Sal Vintone's plane is here, and Hanjo Lu's." Evarita shot Uncle Mark a look.

"All animal dealers," Uncle Mark said.

"What are they all doing here?!" Spencer asked. As soon as the words left his mouth, he knew *exactly* what all those animal dealers were doing here. They were here for Pam's party. The very party Bearhaven's team had planned its whole mission around.

B.D. was apparently thinking the same thing. "My guess

is tonight's party is not going to be a happy celebration for Pam's friends and family," he said.

Spencer reached for the jade bear in his pocket, hoping to calm his racing mind. But when he realized there was nothing there, Spencer's stomach flipped over. The jade bear was still lost in Bearhaven.

"So there will be some illegal animal dealers at Hidden Rock Zoo when we arrive tonight?" Aldo asked. The bear sounded hopeful, like maybe Evarita could offer another explanation.

Evarita sighed. "Unfortunately, I think Hidden Rock Zoo is going to be *swarming* with illegal animal dealers and all kinds of unsavory characters tonight."

"I say we move forward as planned," Uncle Mark said. Spencer looked at him. His usually blond uncle had tucked his wavy hair into a perfectly gelled dark brown wig. His eyebrows jutted out much farther than they normally did, and his nose was bigger. Uncle Mark was totally transformed. He went on, "Whether or not the party is for animal dealers, it will still give us a way into Hidden Rock Zoo, and a distraction for the mission once we're in."

"I agree," B.D. said.

"All right." Evarita shut her laptop and put it aside. "The catering truck is already here anyway, and I'd hate to see you waste your disguise, Mark." She raised an eyebrow, looking at Uncle Mark.

"You can call me Alfonso," Uncle Mark replied.

Spencer laughed, and the tension in the plane seemed to lift a little bit.

"Now your turn, Spence." Uncle Mark handed Spencer a wig and a pair of angular black glasses.

Spencer tugged the wig down over his own shaggy brown hair and slipped on the glasses. He turned back to the mirror Uncle Mark had propped up in one of the drawers. Between the shoulder-length blond hair, the glasses, and the white chef's jacket he had already changed into, he barely recognized himself.

"You can call me Rex," he said, picking the first thing that came to mind.

Uncle Mark chuckled. "You got it, Rex. Evarita, will you help B.D. and Aldo switch from BEAR-COMs to Ear-COMs?" Uncle Mark nodded toward the translating devices around the bears' necks. Spencer knew the BEAR-COMs had to be left behind on the plane with Evarita. The bears would switch to the more discreet technology, the Ear-COMs, for the mission ahead. Spencer lifted a hand and adjusted his own Ear-COM, the one Professor Weaver had made just for him, adapted from an old Ear-COM of Mom's. It fit into his ear just like a hearing aid would.

"Of course," Evarita answered.

"Come on, Rex." Uncle Mark started toward the door. "We'll get the truck ready."

Spencer followed Uncle Mark out of the plane and down to the ground where a catering truck Evarita said had been delivered by "a friend to Bearhaven" was parked.

Creative Pastry was printed in swirly black letters on the sides of the catering truck. Uncle Mark opened the back doors.

23

The far end of the truck was taken up by a huge fridge. Spencer could see through the fridge's glass doors to an enormous, three-tiered cake. Glass bottles of milk and cream filled the remaining shelves. The rest of the truck was lined with rolling carts piled high with smaller desserts.

"Are these real?" Spencer asked, reaching for a mini chocolate mousse from a nearby tray. In the center of the chocolate treat was a dark chocolate disk imprinted with a golden bear. The chocolate mousses looked decadent—and expensive. But most of all, they looked like something Pam would definitely want to serve at his party.

"You bet," Uncle Mark answered. "Evarita had them made by a pastry chef a few towns over from here."

Spencer put the chocolate mousse back on its tray. "Where will the bears and Mom and Dad hide?" He looked around the truck. This was supposed to be their getaway vehicle at the end of the mission.

Uncle Mark climbed into the truck. He went to one of the fridge doors and pulled it open, revealing a big empty space.

"But . . ." Spencer started, confused. Where were the milk jugs? And the cake? Uncle Mark closed the door again, and they reappeared.

"The doors are a foot thick, glass in the front, and a screen in the back playing an image of the inside of a fridge," Uncle Mark explained. He opened the door to the fridge again.

"But it looks so real!" Spencer exclaimed.

"That's the idea."

"Team." Evarita's voice was suddenly in Spencer's ear,

coming loud and clear through the Ear-COM. "We're all set up here."

Now that Evarita had said *Team*, his Ear-COM would be connected to hers, B.D.'s, Aldo's, and Uncle Mark's until one of them said *Disconnect*. By now, Spencer was used to the technology. He knew if the whole team communication was disconnected, and he wanted to speak to any one member of the team, he'd say just their name and their Ear-COMs alone would connect.

"Great, we're ready for you," Uncle Mark said. He stepped to one side of the open fridge door. A moment later, B.D. descended the stairs from the plane to the catering truck in a few long strides. Aldo followed, and Uncle Mark closed them into the fake fridge.

Evarita came to stand beside Spencer. "Good luck." She gave his shoulder a squeeze.

"Thanks." Spencer forced a smile. He tried to block out the rows of menacing, empty planes around them. *We're probably going to need it.*

6

Uncle Mark pulled the Creative Pastry truck onto a narrow paved road marked *Hidden Rock Zoo, Private Property*. Spencer spotted a black Rolls-Royce up ahead, following the dark lane as it wound closer and closer to a looming stone wall.

Headlights flashed into the passenger-side mirror. Spencer tried to see who had pulled in behind them, but the bright lights got into his eyes and he had to look away.

"There's someone behind us," he said, feeling uneasy.

"That's a good thing," Uncle Mark answered. "The guards will spend less time on us if there's a guest waiting to get in."

They drove around a bend in the lane, and the front gates of Hidden Rock Zoo came into sight. The gates were made of iron and wood—two massive, solid doors that, when they were closed, wouldn't allow so much as a glimpse of the property beyond. The gates stood open now, though, with a guardhouse beside them. Two burly-looking guards in black uniforms stared out at the three incoming vehicles.

Uncle Mark slowed their catering truck to a stop as the Rolls-Royce pulled up to the guards. The two guards stepped around to either side of the car, scrutinizing the passengers and checking a clipboard that the guard on the left was holding. A moment later, the Rolls was waved through the gates. Uncle Mark pulled up and rolled down his window.

Spencer stared at the black button-down shirt the guard closest to him was wearing, avoiding the guard's eyes. *Hidden Rock Security* was stitched in silver thread on the guard's chest. Below the words, the silhouette of a crown had been embroidered.

"Name?" the guard closest to Uncle Mark asked.

"Alfonso Rioal, from Creative Pastry," said Uncle Mark.

"Caterers already arrived," the guard answered flatly.

"We've just got the special-order dessert," Uncle Mark answered. He sounded completely calm.

"Guy, you know anything about a special dessert?" the guard beside Uncle Mark called, searching the paper on the clipboard in front of him. The guard near Spencer, who must be Guy, walked back around the truck to stand with his partner.

"No," Guy replied with a shrug.

"All right," Uncle Mark said, acting as though he was trying to be patient. "Well, I've got a three-tiered cake and two hundred custom mini chocolate mousses in the back. Already paid for."

The guards exchanged a look. Guy glanced at the car behind the Creative Pastry truck. "What's the kid doing here?" he asked, returning his attention to Uncle Mark.

"The kid?" Uncle Mark looked over at Spencer. "Oh, him? He's the chocolate taster. A prodigy. He has the best chocolate senses of anyone in the business." Spencer nodded stiffly at each guard, afraid to say anything and accidentally blow his own cover. They stared blankly back at him, obviously uncertain about whether or not to believe that there was such a thing as a chocolate taster in the first place.

"But, anyway, can we drop off the dessert or not?" Uncle Mark pressed on. "Like I said, these specialty chocolates are paid for, so whether I take this delivery where it's supposed to go or you turn me away and I take it back doesn't make much difference to me."

"Guy, start clearing the next car," the guard nearest Uncle Mark said. "I'm gonna check their truck."

Uncle Mark swung his door open and hopped down from the driver's seat. Spencer stayed frozen where he was, listening to Uncle Mark unlatch the back door of the truck. He felt the truck dip a little as someone climbed into the back. He held his breath.

Just then, Guy called out, "This car is clear."

The truck dipped again. Whoever had climbed into the back—Spencer guessed it was the guard—had jumped back out.

"All right, go ahead."

Yes!

Uncle Mark climbed back into the driver's seat.

"Thanks." He nodded at the guards, then pulled through the gates into Hidden Rock Zoo.

Uncle Mark steered them through what seemed to be a tunnel made of trees. Straight ahead, an enormous, sparkling fountain stood at the entrance to Pam's estate. There were five metallic bears, four of them golden, standing on all fours.

Each one faced a different direction, and spouted water from its mouth. In the middle of the four gold bears, a silver bear, twice as big, stood up on its hind legs. Spencer shuddered. It looked like the bear was glaring at him, ready to attack. There was a crown on top of the silver bear's enormous head. A geyser of water shot out from each of the crown's points. Spotlights were trained on the fountain from all directions, and the gushing water reflected the light in harsh beams. Spencer had to look away.

The road they were on forked in opposite directions. The fork to the left was the darker of the two, leading out into what looked like a big open field. Spencer squinted into the dark. Mom and Dad were here somewhere. They could be just a few yards away for all Spencer knew! He strained his eyes, desperate to see *something*.

"I think we go right," Uncle Mark muttered. He turned right, passing a parking lot filled with gleaming, expensive cars. The Rolls-Royce that had arrived ahead of the Creative Pastry truck pulled in between a Bentley and a Lamborghini. Spencer watched a woman step out of the driver's seat of the Rolls-Royce. She was wearing a long white dress and a fur vest, even though it was way too hot for any kind of coat.

"Team," Uncle Mark said, connecting his own Ear-COM with Spencer's, Aldo's, B.D.'s, and Evarita's. "We're in. Can everyone hear me all right?"

"Yeah," Spencer said first.

"I can hear you," Aldo's voice sounded in Spencer's ear.

"Yes," B.D. said.

The Ear-COMs fell silent.

"Evarita, can you hear me?" Uncle Mark said. The Ear-COMs were silent again. "Evarita?" Still nothing. "We don't seem to have a connection with Evarita."

No connection with Evarita? No connection with Evarita meant no connection with the outside world . . . Spencer started to reach for his jade bear, then stopped himself, remembering again with a sinking feeling that it wasn't there.

Uncle Mark pulled into a small parking lot. There were three catering trucks in the dimly lit lot, but the catering staff all seemed to be somewhere else. There was no one in sight. "There must be a kitchen the caterers are working out of," Uncle Mark explained. "That's a good thing. We won't seem suspicious if we park here, but we won't have to worry about a bunch of waiters and cooks poking around, either." Uncle Mark parked the Creative Pastry truck alongside one of the real caterer's vehicles.

"What about Evarita?" Spencer asked, afraid to hear Uncle Mark's answer.

"I'm about to figure that out." Uncle Mark pulled his black backpack onto his lap. He took out a small device Spencer didn't recognize. Uncle Mark turned the device on. It immediately started to beep, and a red light flashed on and off. After a second, the device stopped beeping, and the red light stopped flashing. It just stayed on, like a miniature stoplight.

"The red light means it can't detect any signals nearby. Pam must have signal blockers surrounding the place," Uncle Mark said. "Nobody's going to be able to transmit any information into or out of Hidden Rock Zoo tonight. I don't know if the blocking is permanent or just turned on tonight for the party, but we're not going to be able to connect with Evarita as long as Pam's signal blockers are on."

"But why?" Spencer asked.

"To stop people like us, Spence. And anyone else who might want to know what he's up to in here. It makes it much harder to spy on someone when they jam up your gear like this."

"All right, no Evarita tonight." B.D.'s impatient voice broke into the conversation. "Mark, you should get moving."

"Right." Uncle Mark snapped to attention. "We can't get sidetracked. Come on, Spence, let's see what we're working with." Uncle Mark got out of the truck and closed the door behind himself. Spencer pushed his glasses into place and jumped out to join his uncle.

The parking lot backed up to a wall of trees and bushes. A single path led through the wall, and beyond it Spencer could see there was an elaborate garden. He wanted to see more, but he couldn't without getting closer.

"I'm going in to find Dora," Uncle Mark said quietly. He headed back toward the truck, unbuttoning his chef's coat and slipping it off as he walked. Spencer knew this was the first step in the plan: rescue Dora, then use her knowledge of Hidden Rock Zoo to find Mom and Dad. But he hadn't realized that plan meant he would be left behind in the truck.

"What about me?" he asked, stepping away from the entrance to the garden.

Uncle Mark walked around to the back of the truck and opened it. A light popped on and spilled out into the shadowy parking lot. Spencer watched as his uncle traded the white chef's coat for a black tuxedo jacket, transforming himself with the help of his second disguise that day. With an empty silver tray tucked under one arm, Uncle Mark had gone from a chef to a waiter.

"You have to stay here and guard the truck. Start filling the silver trays with chocolate mousse." Spencer looked blankly back at his uncle. *Guard the truck?* "Just look busy," Uncle Mark went on. "And if you see someone coming, or you have any trouble and need help, I'll be able to hear you on the Ear-COM. The code word is 'peanut butter.'"

7

Spencer placed ten miniature chocolate mousses on a silver tray one by one, just as Uncle Mark had instructed. He was standing in the back of the Creative Pastry truck, less than five feet from the trick doors to the fridge where Aldo and B.D. were hidden, trying to convince himself to keep doing what Uncle Mark had told him to do: guard the truck. It wasn't going very well. With every second that ticked by, Spencer became more certain that by arranging tiny desserts on a silver tray he wasn't helping anyone. And he *definitely* wasn't getting any closer to finding Mom and Dad.

Spencer put the tray down and jumped out of the catering truck. He closed the door behind himself almost all the way, leaving it open a crack so B.D. and Aldo wouldn't be trapped inside if there was an emergency.

He looked around the empty parking lot, convinced he was doing the right thing. After all, a long-haired kid moving bear-imprinted chocolates around an empty catering truck was *way* more suspicious than an empty catering truck in a row of other empty catering trucks. And Spencer *had* made major discoveries every time he'd taken matters into his own hands before. Getting out of the truck now seemed like the exact right thing to do. Uncle Mark had gone into the party to search for Dora, but nobody had gone in to gather information and scout the place. What if Spencer discovered something that led them to Mom and Dad more quickly, or something to help them protect Bearhaven?

Spencer grabbed his mission pack from the front seat of the truck and crept over to the path leading into the garden. He couldn't walk right into the party the way Uncle Mark had. There was no way Spencer would be able to pass for a waiter. He'd have to make sure he wasn't seen. Spencer took off his white chef's coat. He rolled it up and stuffed it inside his mission pack, then swung the black backpack onto his back over his dark gray T-shirt. He could do it—keep himself invisible—he just had to use everything he'd learned in Bear Stealth training.

Spencer searched the small section of garden that he could see from the shadowy parking lot. He narrowed his eyes, slipping into operative mode. There was a row of flowering bushes not far away. He dropped to his hands and knees, and scrambled as fast as he could into the garden. His heart started to beat faster the moment he broke out of the darkness. The pure white pebbles of the path dug into his palms as he pushed himself in between two flowering bushes.

Okay, calm down, he thought. Spencer was careful not to let a sound escape his lips, afraid it would be sent straight to Uncle Mark's Ear-COM, revealing that Spencer had left the truck. He pushed a branch of pink flowers out of his face and took a better look around the garden. He had to admit, it was pretty cool. The path of white pebbles was lined in blazing lanterns as it wound in and out of lush greenery. Exotic flowers Spencer had never seen before seemed to be in bloom everywhere, and marble bridges arched over a crystal clear stream.

Spencer's eyes followed the stream. It created a moat around a wide marble courtyard, where tables and chairs were set up for the party. Off to one side, an orchestra was playing. The music almost drowned out the rushing sound of the waterfall, which was *definitely* the coolest thing in the garden. The towering wall of water started high above the garden, so high Spencer couldn't see what was beyond it. All he could see at the top of the waterfall were two sculptures. Each sculpture was of a bear on all fours, crouching, its eyes trained on the scene below. The bears looked like they were made of water themselves, but Spencer guessed they were glass.

"Have you seen him yet?"

Spencer froze. Two people were walking down the path toward him. The blazing lanterns illuminated their faces. One of them was the woman in the white dress, from the Rolls. Her blond hair was pulled back tightly, and her eyebrows were furrowed in what looked to Spencer like a permanent glare. The man with her wore a black suit, and a black hat that hid his eyes. He wore a silver ring on each of his fingers. Each of his nine fingers. Spencer looked away from the man's right hand, where the pinkie ended in a scar-covered nub.

"No, not yet," the woman answered. "I've never met him at all actually. What's the best way to get into his good graces?"

The man chuckled. "Compliment him."

They must be talking about Pam, Spencer thought.

"Any ideas where the new inventory is coming from?" the woman asked.

New inventory? Spencer gulped. That could only mean one thing: Pam had a bunch of bears he wanted to sell.

"No, I haven't got a clue. But I want a piece of it."

"From the way the invitation put it, it sounds like there's going to be plenty to go around, Lucian."

Lucian! Spencer tried not to gasp. The man with nine fingers must be Lucian Line, the owner of *Hook, Line, and Skinner.* Spencer shrank back even deeper into the bushes.

"As a rule, I don't buy anything I can't have right away," Lucian said, confirming Spencer's fears. "But Pam always delivers."

The woman didn't answer. Spencer was careful to stay completely still as the two animal dealers passed his hiding spot and continued down the path. Before Spencer could try to make any sense of what he'd overheard, a deep, loud gong sounded, making him jump. He turned his attention to the marble courtyard, where everyone was moving around the tables, finding their seats. A woman held her empty glass out into the air until a waiter rushed up to take it. The waiter was Uncle Mark. He obviously hadn't found Dora yet. But Spencer wasn't surprised. Pam didn't seem to be here, and they knew Pam liked to keep the bear close to him. If Pam wasn't here, Dora wouldn't be here, either.

Spencer thought he saw a flash of movement in the shadows to one side of the waterfall. He squinted, trying to make out what it was. A hulking figure stepped out of the dark. Then a hand reached out and snatched the large figure back. If Spencer hadn't known any better, he would have thought it was a bear, but it wasn't. The man who was just pulled back into the shadows was Ivan Lalicki, and the angry hand could only have belonged to his sister, Margo.

Spencer shrank even deeper into his hiding spot between the two flowering bushes. If Margo and Ivan caught sight of him, he didn't think his blond wig and glasses would save him from being recognized. And if Margo and Ivan found him now, this mission to rescue Mom and Dad could be over before it even had a chance to begin.

8

The orchestra music cut out, leaving only the sound of the waterfall crashing and the chatter of the party guests.

"Welcome, friends," a high-pitched voice filled the garden. It was Pam, speaking through a loudspeaker from somewhere Spencer couldn't see.

The light in every lantern in the garden went out—all their flames extinguished at once. Only the marble courtyard with its candlelit tables and sparkling lights, and the spot-lit waterfall, were illuminated now.

Spencer searched the courtyard for Pam from the safety of the darkened garden as all the guests did the same thing. Many of them were turning in their chairs, looking for their host, but he wasn't in the courtyard. Spencer turned back to the waterfall. What had Margo and Ivan been up to over there?

Kaboom!

Spencer jumped, startled, as two fireworks shot up over the waterfall. Each one screamed straight up in the air, showering white sparks over the glass bears. At the top of their flight, they exploded into a pinwheel display. In the same instant as the final explosion, the waterfall disappeared.

The water that had been pouring down from some unknown source stopped, leaving the two glass bears staring down over a shining black wall. Spencer thought he heard a gasp from the courtyard. The image of a silver crown was projected onto the wall, and directly below it, standing in the center of the spotlight, was Pam. A jet-black bear sat back on its haunches beside him.

Dora.

Applause broke out over the marble courtyard. Pam waved back at his guests. He looked horribly pompous. And horribly evil. When the clapping stopped, Pam took a theatrical bow. "I'm so *very* glad you all accepted my invitation," he crooned. "I am on the verge of making history!" Pam paused, a smug smile on his face. He wore a dark purple shirt under a silky black tuxedo. It matched the shiny, oily black hair that fell in a perfect wave over his forehead. And even though Spencer was too far away to see Pam's fingers, he knew that each one ended with a long, clawlike nail. Spencer had seen those disgusting talons twice before. Pam reached out a hand and stroked Dora's head, and Spencer shuddered, imagining those fingernails running through the bear's fur.

Spencer saw some of the guests exchange looks, impressed, he guessed, by Pam's control over an unrestrained bear, especially one as large and powerful looking as B.D.'s sister.

"No one has *ever* had access to the number of high-caliber bears that I am about to bring to the market," Pam announced. An even louder round of applause broke out in the courtyard. Spencer bit his lip, furious there were so many people who could mistreat bears the way Pam did, buying and selling them like cars.

"Tonight, you are in luck," Pam went on.

Dora huffed loudly beside him. She swung her head from side to side with her nostrils flared. She was smelling for something, Spencer could tell.

Pam tensed slightly beside her, but he went on in his disturbingly sweet voice, as though Dora's huffs were all part of the act. "Now, Dora, we can't keep *all* those beautiful bears for ourselves." He stroked her head again. "My friends, each and every one of you have an *exclusive* opportunity to participate in tonight's advance sale. And I assure you, the inventory you are about to preview will not disappoint."

There was a third—even louder—round of applause. Just as the clapping started to quiet, the silver crown on the black wall behind Pam was replaced by new images.

NO! Spencer squeezed his eyes shut, and his heart started to pound in his chest. He opened his eyes to look at the pictures again, desperate to be wrong about what he'd seen there. But the images were the same.

The "inventory" Pam was allowing the most dangerous animal traders in the world to preview tonight was made up of bears, but not just any bears. Bearhaven's bears. B.D., Aldo, Kate, Yude, and Ro Ro, the first bear Spencer had ever helped rescue, were five of the six bears whose images were projected onto the wall behind Pam. Spencer's eyes blurred with furious tears.

He searched for Uncle Mark, who was still posing as a waiter, in the courtyard. Even in the candlelight, and even with prosthetics hiding Uncle Mark's face, Spencer could tell his uncle's expression was grim. Spencer thought of Aldo and B.D., hiding in the Creative Pastry truck not far from here. If this mission didn't go well . . . Spencer tried to push the thought away, but the danger B.D., Aldo, and all of Bearhaven's bears were in had suddenly gotten a lot more real. And a lot more terrifying.

"Without further ado, let's preview the wares and start the auction, shall we?" Pam chirped, his sickly sweet voice still blasting out over a loudspeaker.

Auction? Spencer's stomach flopped again. Pam was going to sell these bears tonight, deciding their doomed fates, before he even had them in his possession. But how could Pam auction off Bearhaven's bears—B.D., Aldo, Kate, Yude, and Ro Ro—before he even knew where the bears lived? Before he had even discovered Bearhaven's location? Spencer took a deep breath. *Either Pam is crazy for selling these bears now, or he's a whole lot closer to taking over Bearhaven than we realized,* Spencer thought.

The images projected behind Pam dissolved and were replaced by a new photo. Now only B.D.'s image showed on the sleek black surface. The picture looked like it had been taken a long time ago. The bear was younger, and he looked much less healthy and powerful than the B.D. Spencer knew now. In the back of the picture, Spencer could see something green and gold—it was too blurry to make out—but the colors were enough for Spencer to guess that the picture had been taken at Gutler University, before B.D.'s rescue.

"We have a bear of unparalleled stature," Pam announced cheerfully as the soundtrack of a bear attacking something was played out over the garden. "This bear's size and musculature will amaze you." Suddenly, another image appeared beside B.D.'s. It was the one bear Spencer didn't recognize. Pam glared off to one side of the waterfall-turned-stage. Spencer followed his gaze and could just make out Margo and Ivan there. Margo was holding a clipboard, and beside her, Ivan seemed to be holding something else. Margo elbowed Ivan sharply. *He must be controlling the slideshow,* Spencer guessed.

"Brothers," Pam practically squealed with joy, returning his attention to his horrible sale. "The pair can be purchased together. And trust me, my friends, their brotherhood and training in entertainment makes the set an incredible *investment.*"

John Shirley. Spencer stared up at the picture of B.D. and Dora's brother, the third Benally sibling. Spencer had never met John Shirley. After his successful rescue from Gutler, the bear had chosen to live in the wild.

Wait a second! Pam thinks John Shirley is in Bearhaven! Spencer realized with some relief. He'd been afraid Pam had forced Mom and Dad to give him information about Bearhaven. Spencer knew Mom and Dad would *never* tell Pam anything willingly, but he didn't trust Pam not to force Mom and Dad to talk. Spencer didn't have to worry about that now, though. Pam thought John Shirley lived in Bearhaven, and John Shirley didn't, and all Pam's photos were out-of-date. He didn't know any more about Bearhaven than their team had thought.

There was a flash of lights, and the photos of B.D. and John Shirley were replaced with a shot of Yude, Bearhaven's key strategist who always wore his green cloak wrapped around him and who Spencer had only recently started to get along with. The image was grainy and had obviously been taken from one of the security cameras at Pam's Moon Farm factory.

"Tonight you'll also have the chance to win the rights to own this male," Pam cheered. "His intelligence is virtually unparalleled in the ursine species." After another flash of lights, Kate was on the screen. Spencer gritted his teeth. A video of the cub, Spencer's best friend in Bearhaven, played for the animal dealers in the garden. Spencer had to look away. He couldn't stand to see Kate chained up at Moon Farm again. "A cub with endless potential and a coat that will one day be worth thousands." Another flash showed Ro Ro. "A mother bear will afford you countless flawless cubs." Pam paused, obviously waiting for something. Nothing happened. He shot another angry glance in Margo and Ivan's direction. A moment later, a picture of Ro Ro's cubs appeared on the screen. They were snuggled together in the ramshackle shed that Spencer had rescued them from.

"And finally . . ." Pam boomed. Lights flashed over the garden, and an image of Aldo filled the wall behind Pam. Spencer felt a lump rise in his throat. "A young bear whose strength and majesty are already undeniable."

Dora huffed. Spencer tore his eyes away from Aldo up on the screen to look at Dora. Pam exploded in a gleeful, high-pitched laugh. "No, Dora, not more majestic than you, of course. But *almost*." He looked out at his guests and gave a dramatic, disgusting wink. "We'll start the auction with this one," Pam announced in a voice that made Spencer flinch it was so giddy. He waved a clawed hand up at the picture of Aldo. "Bid high, friends!" he cheered.

We won't let him get away with this, Spencer promised himself.

Kaboom! Another set of fireworks exploded up from behind the glass bears, spiraling loudly into the night sky.

Pam and Dora moved out of the spotlight. They crossed one of the marble bridges to the courtyard. Pam started to weave around the crowded tables, waving and smiling, but Dora stayed behind on the bridge. She rose up onto her hind legs, swinging her head back and forth, smelling the air. Behind her, Margo stepped out of the shadows. She was holding the clipboard and clutching a microphone. She had one of her usual ugly sneers on her face, and she wore a black tuxedo jacket with a gold bear embroidered on the chest. Her straggly greenish-blond hair had been combed into a bun on top of her head, but it didn't make her look any more professional, just more mean.

"Bidding for this strong and majestic bear starts at ten thousand dollars," Margo croaked.

Immediately, guests in the courtyard lifted their hands into the air. The auction for Aldo had begun, but Spencer ignored it. He kept his eyes on Dora, who had returned to all fours and was padding around the edge of the courtyard. She crossed the marble bridge closest to Spencer and loped into the dark.

9

"I see Dora," Uncle Mark's voice sounded in Spencer's ear.

"Where is she?" B.D. answered immediately.

"She's heading for the parking lot where you are. So am I."

Spencer gave the courtyard one last glance. He saw Uncle Mark drop back into the shadows. Nobody seemed to be paying attention to the phony waiter. All of Pam's guests had their eyes locked on Margo, who was rattling off numbers and pointing into the crowded courtyard, running the auction for the rights to own Aldo as soon as he was captured. The price was climbing. Spencer heard Pam laugh. He found the potbellied man in the center of the courtyard, smiling gleefully.

Spencer had seen enough. He crept out of his hiding spot between the two flowering bushes. All the flames in the lanterns that had lit the garden earlier were still extinguished. Spencer snuck back down the white pebbled path in what felt like total darkness. He took one step into the dimly lit parking lot and immediately stopped.

"She's here," B.D. said, echoing Spencer's thought. Dora was there, standing just a few paces away from the Creative Pastry truck. "I can smell her."

Spencer heard someone rushing up behind him. He spun around, relieved that it was Uncle Mark.

"What's going on?" Uncle Mark whispered urgently. Spencer pointed into the parking lot at Dora, afraid to draw her attention.

"I think she smells B.D, too," he whispered.

Dora rose up onto her hind legs. She batted the back door of the Creative Pastry truck with one of her front paws. A second later, the door swung open, and B.D. jumped out of the truck. Dora shuffled back a few paces.

Spencer and Uncle Mark looked on in silence. B.D. and Dora hadn't seen each other since they'd both been in captivity at Gutler University. Spencer knew how long B.D. had hoped to find her. His parents had only been missing for three weeks, and Spencer didn't think he would really feel like his whole self again until they were together. He couldn't imagine what B.D. must feel like now.

"Dora." B.D.'s voice broke the silence. He stepped toward his sister, but again she shuffled back a few paces. Even in the dimly lit parking lot, Spencer could see there was a softness to B.D. he didn't recognize. The bear's voice was different, gentler. "We've searched for you for so long."

Dora stayed silent, her eyes locked on B.D. After a long moment, she made a long, low series of grunts.

"We never meant to leave you," B.D. answered. "We didn't know what was going on any more than you did."

Dora growled a response, but it ended with a jaw pop. *That's a bad sign,* Spencer thought, and for the first time, he realized B.D.'s reunion with Dora wasn't going to go as well as any of them had expected.

"We would never have gotten on the truck if we'd known you wouldn't be there with us." B.D. was trying to explain what had happened at Gutler University, the night Mom, Dad, and Uncle Mark had tried to save the three Benally siblings. Dora was supposed to be the last bear loaded onto the truck, but alarms had sounded before she made it and, with guard dogs approaching, Dora had been too afraid to move. The rescue team had to leave her behind.

Pop! Dora made the jaw-popping sound again. Spencer looked at Uncle Mark, worried. Jaw popping was one of the ways bears showed aggression. Dora was mad.

"We're here to save you now."

Pop! Pop!

"Dora, believe me."

Dora responded with a huffing sound. She puffed air out of her snout angrily.

"B.D., maybe you'd better give her some space," Uncle Mark said. He knew as well as Spencer and B.D. did, Dora was showing all the signs of a bear on the verge of attacking.

But B.D. ignored the warning. He took another step toward his sister. She smacked the ground with one of her front paws and huffed.

"B.D.," Uncle Mark tried to warn the bear again. Spencer looked over his shoulder, afraid someone might hear.

"I'm not leaving you here, Dora. We came to bring you home."

Dora chuffed and thrust her face into B.D.'s. Still, he didn't back away. Dora let out a long, loud bellow and swiped at him with one of her front paws.

"B.D.!" Spencer cried when Dora's claws made contact with the bear's shoulder.

"Quiet," Uncle Mark ordered.

Suddenly, Aldo jumped out of the back of the truck. He popped his jaw, heading for Dora.

"Aldo, stay out of—" B.D. started. He broke off his sentence when Dora lashed out at him again. She tore into B.D.'s leg with her claws.

"B.D.," Uncle Mark said, "let's get out of here."

"Dora, I know—" B.D. words were cut off by another attack. Dora had thrown herself onto B.D. She was biting and clawing at him, but B.D. wouldn't fight back.

"Mark, what do I do?" Aldo asked. His voice sounded as desperate as Spencer felt.

"B.D., we can't sacrifice the mission—" Uncle Mark didn't finish his sentence.

Over the sound of Dora biting and slashing at B.D., Spencer heard the sounds of footsteps on gravel. Someone was coming.

Uncle Mark immediately sprang into action. "Aldo, get the Ear-COM out of B.D.'s ear," he demanded.

Aldo lunged forward, he batted a paw at B.D.'s head as B.D. turned, trying to avoid another gash from Dora's claws. Spencer saw the small translating device fly onto the pavement between himself and the chaotic tangle of bears. He dove for it, scooping the device up off the ground. He shoved it deep into his pocket.

The sound of footsteps on gravel was getting louder.

Spencer scrambled up from the pavement.

"Aldo, Spencer, get out of here!" Uncle Mark ordered.

"Stay together and hide." Uncle Mark turned to face the path to the garden, as though preparing to hold off whoever was coming. He tore his Ear-COM out of his ear and stomped on it, smashing it to pieces.

"But—" Spencer started. What would happen to B.D.? And Uncle Mark?

"NOW!" Uncle Mark roared. Behind his uncle, Spencer caught a glimpse of Ivan turning down the path.

"Spencer!" Aldo called. The bear was running straight at him. Spencer didn't have time to think. As Aldo raced past, Spencer reached out, grabbed two handfuls of the bear's fur, and leaped onto Aldo's back. The fake glasses of his disguise flew off Spencer's face, clattering to the pavement. Aldo didn't slow down. With Spencer glued to his back, the bear tore out into the dark, racing deeper into Hidden Rock Zoo.

10

Spencer held tight to Aldo as the bear ran through the dark, putting space between them and whatever was happening to B.D. and Uncle Mark right now. Spencer strained to see over Aldo's shoulder, hoping to recognize something from the old Hidden Rock Zoo map. But Pam had lit only the courtyard where his party was being held, creating an eerie, glowing pocket of evil in the middle of the garden, and leaving the rest of the zoo a pitch-black mystery.

Thank goodness bears can see better in the dark than humans, Spencer thought.

"Aldo," he whispered, hoping Aldo would be able to hear him over the sound of his paws hitting the ground. "What's going to happen to them? Will B.D. and Uncle Mark be okay?" The second the words left his lips, he felt Aldo slow down.

"I don't know . . . But I don't feel right about leaving them behind."

Spencer hesitated. Uncle Mark had ordered them to stay together and hide, but he hadn't said where. "Let's go back."

"Not all the way," Aldo said, immediately understanding what Spencer meant. "But we should know what happens to them. Where they're taken." Aldo turned around. He sprinted back the way they'd come. A few minutes later, the dim glow of the parking lot came into view. "Hold on," Aldo whispered. Spencer didn't think he could hold on any more tightly than he already was. Aldo rose onto his hind legs and climbed into a tree. He moved silently up into the branches. "Okay," he said as soon as he'd settled himself. Spencer wrapped his arms around a nearby branch and carefully pulled himself off Aldo, quickly finding footing.

"The bear's hurt!" Uncle Mark's voice rose up out of the parking lot. He was yelling. "You don't need to handle him like that."

"You be *quiet*, or Ivan will make you be quiet," another voice hissed. It was Margo.

Spencer peered through the leafy branches of the tree. In the dark, and with the catering trucks blocking his view, he could only make out a sliver of the scene below, but that was enough to make him understand all the fury he had just heard in Uncle Mark's voice.

Three guards were restraining B.D., working together to chain him up. B.D.'s whole left shoulder glistened with blood where Dora had torn it open. She looked on from several paces away. Spencer couldn't read her expression, but he didn't care to. Right now, Spencer hated Dora. She had tried to kill B.D.

"Get your hands off me. I know how to walk." It was Uncle Mark's voice again, coming from an area of the parking lot Spencer couldn't see.

"Keep your mouth *shut*, or these could be the last steps you ever take," Margo threatened. "Let's go," she ordered.

"They're coming this way," Aldo whispered.

B.D.'s chains rattled as the guards dragged him forward. Spencer clenched his fists. B.D. wasn't resisting the guards. He wasn't pulling against the chains on purpose, but every time he stepped forward on his left leg, he stumbled. Finally, Uncle Mark came into view. He was no longer wearing his wig, and he was flanked by Margo and Ivan. Ivan had a shiny black football helmet on his head—Spencer had never seen the hulking thug without one—and his huge hand was gripping Uncle Mark's arm. Margo strode out ahead of the group. Her straggly hair had started to fall out of the bun on top of her head, and she looked even more haggard and mean than before. Ivan pushed Uncle Mark forward behind Margo, and the guards brought up the rear, dragging the wounded B.D. behind them.

Aldo tensed, and Spencer held his breath. The group was moving toward them, following the very same route Aldo and Spencer had taken to escape before. They passed right below the branches of the tree where Aldo and Spencer were perched together.

Don't look up . . . Don't look up . . .

Nobody looked up. The group disappeared into the dark. When Uncle Mark, B.D., and their captors were out of sight, Spencer started to move out of the tree. He and Aldo had to follow the group! They had to know where Uncle Mark and B.D. were being taken! Maybe Margo and Ivan would even lead them right to Mom and Dad and this mission wouldn't have to be a disaster. Aldo reached out a paw, stopping Spencer from jumping down.

"What's—" Spencer started, but the bear jerked his head

in the direction of the parking lot, and Spencer swallowed his words. *Dora.* She was still there. The bear sat back on her haunches. They couldn't climb down now. She would see them. Dora wasn't happy to see them like they'd thought she would be—she was vicious. There was no telling what she would do if she discovered them hiding in the tree. But they couldn't lose track of B.D. and Uncle Mark! "What do we do?" Spencer whispered.

"I don't think we have much of a choice," Aldo answered. "We can't go anywhere until she moves."

Spencer glared down at the bear in the parking lot. She bent her head to the pavement and sniffed at a splatter of her brother's blood. *It's your blood, too!* Spencer wanted to yell at her. But he didn't. He crossed his arms and leaned back against the tree to wait.

11

After what felt like hours, Dora padded out of the parking lot.

"Finally," Aldo growled.

"I thought she'd never leave." Spencer swung his backpack off his back. In the eternity they had just spent watching Dora brood in the parking lot, waiting for her to move on, he had mentally reviewed the contents of his mission pack. There was nothing in his pack that would help them get rid of Dora, but he had remembered the night-vision goggles he'd taken from Bearhaven's plane.

Spencer pulled the blond wig off his head and stuffed it to the bottom of his mission pack. There was no point being disguised now. Since Uncle Mark's cover was blown, Margo, Ivan, and Pam would all guess who he was, with or without a wig and glasses. Now Spencer and Aldo just had to stay hidden completely. He pulled out the night-vision goggles, zipped his mission pack back up, and slung it back onto his shoulders. "We'd better hurry," he said, getting ready to return to the ground at last.

Aldo climbed down quickly from the tree. The moment the bear reached the ground, he rose onto his hind legs, turning his head from side to side as he tried to smell B.D. and Uncle Mark or pick up any clues about where they'd been taken.

Spencer could barely see the branch he was sitting on it was so dark. He pulled the night-vision goggles down over his eyes, and his view was totally transformed. He could finally see that Hidden Rock Zoo was more than an inky black desert surrounding Pam's gardens. Buildings, pathways, trees, and fences all materialized through the special lenses of the goggles. And everything was green. Spencer looked down at Aldo. The bear looked like he was glowing. *This is so cool,* Spencer thought, then caught himself. Now was *not* the time to get distracted by spy gear.

Spencer jumped down to the ground from one of the tree's lower branches. With the night-vision goggles, he was too fascinated by everything he was seeing glowing green to be afraid of falling. He landed with a soft thud.

Aldo crouched down, and Spencer climbed onto the bear's back. Without a word, Aldo set off at a run down the path they had watched Margo take. To their right, Spencer thought he saw stables, the first thing he recognized from the old Hidden Rock Zoo map. Soon, they came to a glass gazebo. A small pond glittered beside it. The path forked in front of the gazebo and pond, and Aldo paused, smelling in both directions.

"Any idea?" Spencer whispered. Aldo chose the path to the left without answering. They picked up speed, but the path forked again. They had come to a big building that looked like a greenhouse, with clear glass walls. Spencer could see straight into the building through the glass, and there wasn't anyone inside. Aldo went right, then stopped after a few paces and went back to the fork. He took the path forking left. It curled away from the greenhouse-looking building, then led into a grove of trees. Aldo stopped at the tree line.

"I don't know . . ." Aldo said. He sounded defeated.

Two fireworks screeched into the sky in the direction of the party. Spencer and Aldo both flinched. The thick smell of sulfur washed over them, carried across Pam's property by a strong breeze. "Now I'm never going to be able to smell them!" Aldo said. He sounded defeated. "Maybe we should go back to the first fork in the path . . ." Aldo turned back.

Spencer's stomach twisted. *This is bad.* There wasn't any sign of Uncle Mark or B.D. anywhere. There wasn't even any sign of Margo, Ivan, or the guards who had dragged B.D. away.

When Aldo reached the gazebo with the pond beside it, he sniffed every inch of the path where it forked. He paced back and forth. "I can't smell them," he finally said, sounding increasingly anxious.

Spencer took a deep breath. "Okay. It's okay," he said, trying to calm himself and Aldo down. Spencer climbed off Aldo's back. How had things gone so terribly wrong?

"We need a new plan," Aldo said. Spencer could tell the bear was trying to take charge, but Aldo didn't sound confident at all. Spencer was scared, too. They were alone, with no way to communicate with Evarita or anyone else outside Hidden Rock Zoo. Half their team had been captured. Dora, the long-lost bear they had come to rescue, had turned out to be a violent beast, and they still didn't have a single clue as to where Mom and Dad were being held.

Aldo was right, they did need a new plan. But they couldn't stay here, standing in the dark in the middle of the zoo to plot their next move. Besides, Spencer was starving, and Aldo looked exhausted.

"First, we need a hideout." Spencer reached for the Hidden Rock Zoo map Evarita had tucked into the side pocket of his mission pack. He looked for a building on the opposite side of the zoo from Pam's party. "How does the Reptile Lodge sound to you?" he said, pointing out on the map what looked to be the farthest building from the Hidden Rock Zoo entrance.

"Is that the best we can do?" Aldo didn't sound very enthusiastic.

"It's as far away from Pam and Dora as we can get in this place," Spencer answered. "And I haven't seen any zoo animals yet. It doesn't look like Pam is keeping real animals here—other than bears. If we get lucky, there won't be a single snake in the place."

"We aren't exactly on a lucky streak, Spencer," Aldo joked halfheartedly. "But I think you're right. The farther we can get from the party the better. Lead the way."

Spencer set off in the direction of the Reptile Lodge, hoping with all his might Pam hadn't knocked it down, and that there weren't any reptiles waiting for them inside.

12

Spencer stepped up to the door of a long, windowless building. According to the map, they'd found the Reptile Lodge. And for the first time since arriving at Hidden Rock Zoo, something seemed to be going their way. The building didn't look like it had been changed since Pam bought the zoo. There were no bear sculptures or marble stairs, no waterfalls or glass pavilions, nothing that showed Pam cared about the building at all.

For a second, Spencer allowed himself to hope Mom and Dad were inside, that Pam had locked them up in a building he didn't use and left them alone. He pressed an ear to the door, listening. He didn't hear anything. Aldo bowed his head to the ground and sniffed.

"Think it's safe?" Spencer asked.

"I don't smell anyone." Aldo sat back on his haunches. "Let's go."

Spencer agreed. They were both exhausted and hungry, and they really needed a place to hide out for the night. He put his hand on the door handle and pushed. It was unlocked. He let it swing open and peered into the building through the night-vision goggles. It looked like the coast was clear.

Aldo led the way inside. Spencer stepped in behind the bear and closed the door behind them. He scanned the wall beside the door and spotted a light switch. *It's worth a shot . . .* He flipped the switch, and the Reptile Lodge lights came on. Spencer pulled the night-vision goggles down off his eyes to hang around his neck. He was glad the lights in the Reptile Lodge still worked, but he wished they were a little less ominous. Rather than illuminate the one long hall that made up the entire building, the only lights that blinked on were inside the glass animal enclosures that lined the walls. It looked like it was as bright as day inside the reptile habitats, but the hallway was only lit by the glow spilling out of the forgotten enclosures.

Spencer looked around. There was definitely no one here, but more important, and to his great relief, he didn't see a single snake.

"No reptiles," Aldo remarked happily. Apparently checking for snakes was the first thing on Aldo's mind, too. He padded down the long room, peering into the glass cases. It looked like they'd been ignored for ages. The trees and plants inside were long dead, and the little stone pools were bone-dry.

At the far end of the room was a small foyer and exit. When Aldo reached it, he sat down, resting his back against the wall. Spencer caught up to the bear and dropped his mission pack and night-vision goggles to the floor. He slumped down beside Aldo, relieved to set up camp near an exit door, rather than in the middle of the empty snake cases.

For a second, he and Aldo sat side by side in silence. Then Spencer's stomach growled. Aldo's ears twitched at the sound.

"Are you as hungry as I am?" Spencer asked. He unzipped his mission pack and turned it upside down, emptying the contents into a pile on the floor.

"Yes," Aldo answered. "If I'd known we'd end up here tonight, I would have helped myself to some dessert while I was hiding in the catering truck." He eyed Spencer's pile of supplies.

Spencer sifted through the pile, looking for Raymond's fuel bars. He had six altogether.

"This is all we have." He passed three bars to Aldo. Each one was huge for an energy bar—at least twice the size of any granola bar he'd ever seen—but still, three each didn't seem like very many, especially since they didn't know when they'd be leaving Hidden Rock Zoo. "Maybe we shouldn't finish them tonight."

"Two tonight, one in the morning," Aldo answered. "We'll find more food tomorrow somehow if we have to." The bear hesitated, then looked back to Spencer's mission pack contents.

"I don't have any honey if that's what you're looking for," Spencer joked. Aldo was known for his sweet tooth.

Spencer unwrapped his first fuel bar. He looked back at Aldo, wondering if he should offer to unwrap the bear's, but Aldo was already halfway through his first bar, wrapper and all.

"What? Why are you staring at me like that?" Aldo asked. Then his eyes landed on Spencer's unwrapped fuel bar. "Oh, the wrapper is just pressed leaves. It's edible for bears. It's edible for you, too, but you probably won't like it."

"Well, in that case, you can have mine." Spencer handed

over the brittle wrapper and bit into his first fuel bar. It tasted better than he'd expected, like a peanut butter and jelly sandwich and an oatmeal raisin cookie all in one. "Do you think B.D.'s okay?" he asked once he'd finished his first fuel bar. He pulled B.D.'s Ear-COM out of his pocket and added it to the pile of stuff beside his now empty mission pack.

"I hope so," Aldo said. "I never thought his reunion with Dora would go the way it did . . ."

"I know," Spencer answered. "I didn't think *any* of this would go the way it has."

Spencer looked over the supplies he'd dumped out of his mission pack. When he filled the bag back on the plane, he'd felt prepared for anything, an operative with a mission pack full of gear ready for action. But in the Reptile Lodge his pile of supplies looked tiny, and Spencer wasn't sure he even knew how to use half the things he had packed. "I thought we'd be on the way back to Bearhaven with my mom and dad by now," he muttered.

He wanted to feel better knowing he was closer to Mom and Dad than he'd been in weeks. But he didn't feel any better at all. How could they hope to rescue Mom and Dad, *and* B.D. and Uncle Mark, when they didn't even know where anyone was?

"So did I," Aldo said. "But just because the mission hasn't gone the way we'd planned so far, doesn't mean it's over. We won't leave Hidden Rock Zoo without your parents, Spencer. I promise."

But how? Spencer reached for his jade bear, only to remember his pocket was empty. All the worries that were swirling around in Spencer's head got worse.

"Just like we won't leave without B.D. and Mark," Aldo went on. Spencer could tell the bear was gaining confidence as he spoke. Spencer only felt more defeated. All he wanted was to see Mom and Dad again. He wanted to wake up in his bedroom in the morning and have them down the hall, or play a baseball game with his school team, the Cougars, with Dad watching in the stands. He wanted Mom to help him with his homework on a regular school night . . . Would he *ever* get to do those things with Mom and Dad again?

"What's wrong?" Aldo asked after Spencer hadn't answered him.

"What if we're not . . . good enough operatives to save them, Aldo? You and I have only gone on a few missions before. I'm still in training!"

Aldo cocked his head, looking Spencer over.

"Well, we're about to become good enough operatives. We're not going to fail, Spencer, because we can't, because there's too much at stake, and because we're a team. What one of us can't do, the other one can. Right?"

Spencer thought about it. He hated to climb, but climbing came easily to Aldo, and he could carry Spencer on his back. Spencer could hide in places Aldo couldn't, and he had hands, which meant he could work with rope and do all sorts of things Aldo's claws weren't capable of. Aldo was right: They complemented each other as a team. Together, they could do pretty much anything.

"I guess that's true." Spencer fell silent, lost in thought. "But what if making a good team isn't enough this time, Aldo?" he asked after a second.

"Are you a Plain or aren't you?"

Spencer looked at the bear, surprised. "I am."

"Well, I'm a Weaver. And Plains and Weavers are known for something. Disconnect." Aldo turned off the Ear-COMs so he could say his next word in Ragayo. *"Wanmahai."*

"Wanmahai?" Spencer growled back. "Aldo, what is that?"

"It means coming together to build something," Aldo answered. "It means teamwork. And when it comes to Plains and Weavers, teamwork has *always* been enough. Our parents worked together to build Bearhaven, didn't they?"

"Yeah," Spencer answered. Professor Weaver and the BEAR-COM technology he'd created had given Mom, Dad, and Uncle Mark the tools they needed to make their first rescue at Gutler University. Then Spencer's family, Professor Weaver, and B.D. had founded Bearhaven and started rescuing more bears in distress and transporting those bears to safety.

"So we're going to use teamwork to save it," Aldo said. "Just like we're going to use teamwork to save your family and B.D. from Pam tomorrow, or the next day, or whatever day it is that we get them out of here."

"Wanmahai," Spencer repeated. Aldo was right. He didn't know exactly *how* they were going to save everyone and get out of here, but he did know that whatever happened, their *wanmahai* was going to be a whole lot stronger than anyone or anything that tried to stop them.

13

Hissssss.

Spencer woke with a start on the floor of the Reptile Lodge. *Snakes!* was the first thought that popped into his mind. He sat up quickly, throwing the chef's jacket he'd used for a blanket aside, and frantically searched the floor around him for snakes. He didn't see anything, but the hissing continued.

"Aldo," Spencer whispered, waking the bear who had slept on the floor beside him. "Do you hear that?"

Aldo was awake and alert in an instant. His ears immediately began to twitch. He got to all fours, sniffing rapidly. He padded over to the exit door, lowering his snout to the crack at the bottom. "It's coming from out there," he said. "I don't think it's a snake." Aldo stepped back from the door, giving Spencer space to open it a crack.

Spencer opened the door, and heat and sunlight poured into the Reptile Lodge. The green lawn outside was being watered. Spencer closed the door.

"False alarm," he said sheepishly. "It's just a sprinkler system."

"That's okay." Aldo returned to the spot where they'd

slept for his last Raymond's fuel bar. "We should get moving anyway," he said, between bites.

"Yeah." Spencer rolled up his chef's jacket and stuffed it into his mission pack. He gathered the rest of his supplies and packed them up, too. Last night, before falling asleep, he and Aldo had decided the Reptile Lodge would be their home base. If they got separated at any point, it was where they would go to meet. Still, Spencer didn't want to leave anything behind. There was no telling what he would need on the next phase of the mission. He unwrapped his last Raymond's fuel bar and took a bite.

"So where do you think we should start?" Spencer asked. Their first order of business was to locate everyone. Once they knew where Mom and Dad and B.D. and Uncle Mark were being held, they would come up with a plan to free them and get out of Hidden Rock Zoo. He spread the old zoo map out on the floor between himself and Aldo.

"I think we should stick to the perimeter of the zoo." Aldo ran a claw around the border of the map. "And make our way back to the parking lot with the catering trucks. I might be able to pick up some more clues about where Margo and Ivan took B.D. and Mark from there, now that it's daytime."

"All right, let's do it." Spencer popped the last of his Raymond's fuel bar into his mouth and swung his mission pack onto his back. He folded up the map and stuffed it into his pocket.

They returned to the exit door, and Spencer opened it a crack. Aside from the sprinklers, the lawn beside the Reptile Lodge was empty. According to the map, the next section of the zoo on the perimeter was called Alligator Alley. It was made up of a series of pools and ponds where the bigger reptiles would have been held, and was surrounded by a stone wall. Spencer squinted across the lawn between the Reptile Lodge and Alligator Alley. He could just make out a low stone wall. It looked like Alligator Alley might still be intact.

"Okay." He turned back to Aldo. "Let's get to the stone wall. It'll give us some cover, I think, but we have to get across this open lawn first."

Aldo nodded and crouched down beside Spencer. "The faster we move the better, little man."

Spencer climbed onto the bear's back. "Ready," he said as soon as he had a good grip.

Aldo crossed the lawn in ten long strides and leaped over a small stone wall, landing in what must have once been Alligator Alley. He padded quickly and quietly through the old alligator enclosure. It was made to look like a swamp, with tall grasses and droopy, willowy trees. A murky river wound through it.

"I guess he did get rid of all the animals," Spencer whispered.

"That's okay with me," Aldo answered. "I don't really want to run into an alligator right now."

Aldo paused when they came to the stone wall, looking out over the next landscape. It was called the Savanna on the Hidden Rock Zoo map. Again, Spencer didn't see any animals—not that he was hoping they'd have to navigate giraffes and rhinos. Aldo climbed the fence and broke into a run immediately, sticking close to the wooden fence as he flew across the dry grass and dust. Halfway through the Savanna, the next section of the zoo came into view.

Aldo didn't slow his pace. Spencer squeezed his legs, clamping himself tightly to Aldo's back as the bear launched himself straight over the wooden fence, across the small lawn separating the Savanna and the Shetland Pony Shed, and through the open stable doors.

The moment Aldo landed on all fours inside the Shetland Pony Shed, Spencer started to panic. The building was far from abandoned. In fact, the inside had been completely redone. Now it was a luxury garage, filled with the kinds of cars Spencer knew Uncle Mark would love to drive. There wasn't a single pony in sight, but the stables were definitely *not* clear of animals. Instead, worse than any zoo animal they could have stumbled upon, there was Ivan Lalicki.

14

Aldo lunged into the closest stall in the Shetland Pony Shed. Spencer could feel the bear's heart pounding, and his own heart hammering in his chest. Ivan was standing in the open door at the far side of the stables. His back was turned. He hadn't seen them. But Spencer knew if Ivan was here, Margo probably wasn't too far away. Then Spencer heard her.

"What's taking so long, Ivan?" Margo snapped. "We have a flight to catch, and the boss is *not* going to be pleased if we don't tow that stupid truck before we leave. Creative Pastry," she spat. "Ha! Like we wouldn't have seen through that phony business."

Spencer clenched his fists angrily. Margo was wrong. The Creative Pastry front had worked just fine. If it hadn't been for Dora, Bearhaven's team would never have been caught!

"At least now Pam has a full set of bears in the Caves again," Margo added. The sound of footsteps continued. The Lalickis were coming toward Spencer and Aldo. Spencer willed them to stop walking.

"Not for long," Ivan said slowly, his deep voice booming through the stables.

Margo cackled out a loud laugh. "You're right. That bear sold for thirty-five thousand dollars last night. He'll be a bearskin rug before long."

Spencer shuddered. He hadn't told Aldo about the auction. He could hardly stand to think about it, and news of B.D. being sold for thousands of dollars to one of those horrible people at Pam's party made Spencer's stomach twist into knots. They had to get B.D. out of Hidden Rock Zoo, and fast. The footsteps stopped. "Come on, get in the truck," Margo ordered.

Spencer listened to the sound of car doors opening and closing. An engine rumbled on.

"They're leaving," Spencer whispered. Aldo nodded. Once they heard the truck pull out of the Stables, Spencer slid down off Aldo's back. "That was close!" he whispered.

"I'm sorry, I don't know why I ran in here without checking. We were just so exposed in the Savanna—"

"Don't worry," Spencer interrupted Aldo's hushed apology. "They didn't see us. We're still okay." He pulled the Hidden Rock Zoo map out of his pocket.

"What did they say?" Aldo asked. Margo and Ivan's conversation had been a mystery to him. He could only understand humans who were wearing Ear-COMs connected to his own.

Spencer didn't answer right away. He couldn't explain the auction to Aldo and tell him that B.D. had been sold for lots of money. It was too terrible, and he would have to explain that Aldo himself, Professor Weaver, and Kate had all *also* been sold last night. Spencer's hands were shaking as he held the map between them. "They're towing our catering truck, then leaving Hidden Rock Zoo," he finally managed to choke out some words. "And I think Margo gave away B.D.'s location. She said Pam has a full set of bears in the Caves. Look." He pointed to a part of the map labeled *The Caves*. Its illustration showed bear enclosures. "They must be keeping B.D. there."

"It's on the other side of the zoo," Aldo said quietly. He extended a claw and traced it around the map. "We'll have to get around the gardens. I know it's a little risky, but I don't think we should stay in here any longer."

As though on cue, the sound of footsteps echoed through the stables. Someone had just walked into the building. Spencer and Aldo both froze, listening. Whoever it was stopped walking. A minute went by, then another. Spencer and Aldo exchanged a look. Spencer quietly slipped his mission pack off his back. He unzipped the front pocket without a sound and retrieved a little handheld mirror. He crept to the very edge of the stall and poked the mirror out beyond it until it reflected a view of the rest of the stables. As soon as he'd gotten a glimpse of who was in the stables and what they were doing, he pulled the mirror back and returned it to its place in his mission pack.

"It's a guard," he whispered. "He's sitting on a stool at the far entrance. His back is to us, but I don't think we'll be able to get past him without a distraction."

"Okay," Aldo replied, looking around.

They were only ten feet from an open door. They didn't need the guard to be distracted for long, but they couldn't

risk him glancing over his shoulder as they snuck out of the stables.

Spencer crept back to the edge of the stall they were hiding in. Each stall in the building was spotless, its wood gleaming almost as much as the fancy cars and trucks parked inside. Spencer counted the stalls, there were eight on each side, and brand-new-looking vehicles were parked in four of them. Spencer spotted a silver Maserati, and a plan started to take shape in his mind.

"I have an idea," he whispered as he dug into his mission pack for something else. When he pulled out the slingshot, Aldo eyed it with curiosity. Spencer searched the floor. He grabbed a pebble a second later. *Let's hope this works,* he thought,

trying to remember the last time he'd actually used a slingshot. "I'm going to get onto your back, okay? Just be ready to run."

Aldo crouched down. Spencer climbed onto the bear's back, clamping his legs around Aldo's sides. He fit the pebble into the slingshot and took aim at the Maserati. "Ready?" he whispered.

"Ready."

Spencer pulled back the slingshot and let the pebble fly straight at the side of the silver Maserati.

Ping!

Weee oooo weee oooo!

The pebble hit its mark, and the Maserati's alarm immediately started blaring. Spencer grabbed hold of Aldo's fur, getting the best grip he could with the slingshot still in one hand. At the sound of the alarm, the guard leaped up from his seat and ran into the Maserati's stall.

"Now!" Spencer hissed as the guard disappeared into the stall. Aldo flew forward, lunging out of the Shetland Pony Shed. The sound of the alarm drowned out the bear's racing footsteps.

15

Aldo crept along the zoo's outer wall with Spencer on his back. They were taking the long way to the Caves, skirting the entire perimeter of the zoo and passing the guest parking lot, the tree tunnel, and the bear fountain in order to avoid Pam's staff, who were cleaning up. Finally, they were next to an elaborate set of pools. The map had called them the Seaport Pools, and they'd originally been built as separate habitats for penguins, sea lions, and otters, but now they were connected by babbling waterfalls and had lounge chairs and cabanas arranged around their sides.

Between the outer wall of the zoo and the rock formation, there was an alleyway just big enough for Aldo to walk through. Aldo stepped into the shadows of the alley, and Spencer slid off the bear's back. He pulled the zoo map out of his pocket.

"It looks like these rocks open up into eight caves, one for each species of bear." Spencer pointed to the illustration of the Caves. Aldo nodded, agreeing. "I think if we went around the front, we'd be able to see into each enclosure."

"Too risky. Is there a way in back here?" Aldo loped down the alleyway.

"There must be. They have to feed the bears somehow."

"B.D. is definitely nearby. I can smell him." Suddenly, Aldo stopped. He rose onto his hind legs and rested his paws on a door in the rock wall. "Here."

Spencer jogged to catch up with the bear. He stepped in front of Aldo and pushed open the door to reveal a long hallway. They stepped inside, and Spencer closed the door behind them.

"Spencer," Aldo whispered. Spencer looked over his shoulder, then immediately spun around. He backed up until he was pressed against the door he'd just closed. A grizzly bear was staring at them. The sound of the door opening and closing must have gotten his attention. Spencer gulped. Without a BEAR-COM, there was no way to explain to the carnivore that he was there to help.

"It's okay," Aldo said. "He can't get out."

Aldo was right. The grizzly bear was behind glass, locked into his own enclosure. Spencer looked down the hall. The grizzly wasn't the only bear looking at them.

The hallway reminded Spencer of a hospital. It was brightly lit and sterile. All along one side of the hall were shelves filled with supplies. The other side of the hall was a brick wall, broken up every few yards by a metal door, and a floor-to-ceiling glass window. Each door and window marked a new cave, and the entrance to a different bear's enclosure. To the left of the grizzly bear, Spencer saw a polar bear. *Another carnivore.*

Spencer stepped away from the door he was leaning against. He moved closer to the grizzly bear. The animal was huge. Much bigger than Aldo.

"Come on," Aldo said, taking off down the hallway. "We didn't come here to look at bears." Spencer heard the edge in Aldo's voice. He guessed any bear in captivity made Aldo angry. Spencer didn't like thinking about Pam owning the bears in the Caves, either, but he couldn't help being fascinated. He'd only ever seen a black bear up close, never a grizzly or a polar bear. He tore himself away from the grizzly bear's cave and started down the hall after Aldo. He passed the polar bear, then an empty cave. Spencer spotted bamboo through the mouth of the empty cave. *This one must be for a panda,* he thought, hurrying past.

Aldo was in front of the last enclosure in the row. His head was bowed. Spencer ran up to meet him.

"B.D.!" Spencer gasped when he got a glimpse of the head of Bearhaven's Bear Guard. He tried to open the door to B.D.'s cave. They had to get in right away! But the door was locked. Spencer pressed his hands against the glass window. He stared at B.D., desperate to get to him.

Unlike the grizzly and the polar bear, B.D. wasn't sitting back on his haunches, looking out the window of his cave at Aldo and Spencer. Instead, B.D. lay on the cement floor. His face turned to the wall. His fur was clumped with dried blood.

A lump rose in Spencer's throat. "Is he . . . breathing?"

Aldo didn't answer. He moved forward and butted the glass with his head. "B.D.," he said, then launched into a long, low, pleading string of Ragayo. "B.D., wake up. It's me and Spencer. We're here. We're about to get in and help you. Just . . . wake up, B.D."

B.D. stirred. His ears twitched.

"He's alive! He heard you!" Spencer cheered.

B.D. lifted his head. He turned to the window and, at the sight of Aldo and Spencer, struggled to get to all fours. The massive bear seemed to wince with every move he made, but by the time he'd risen to stand, he'd managed to hide any sign of pain.

16

Spencer knelt on the floor outside B.D.'s cave, his eyes narrowed on the locked door. He moved the lock pick and miniature wrench again, jabbing them around in the lock on the enclosure's door. A lock-picking kit was fortunately one of the things he had added to his mission pack on Bearhaven's plane, but unfortunately, one of the things he didn't exactly know how to use.

If only he could communicate with Uncle Mark or Evarita! He was sure one of them would be able to talk him through picking the lock. He glanced down at the instructions that had come with the kit one more time. "Push the pins up with the pick until they set," they said. *Whatever that means . . .*

Aldo was pacing back and forth behind him. "Is it working?"

Spencer glared at the locked door. He adjusted the wrench and wiggled the pin in the lock again.

Click!

"Yes!" Spencer leaped to his feet. He pushed the door open and rushed in to B.D.'s side, only narrowly avoiding being trampled by Aldo.

"B.D.! Are you okay?!" Spencer tried to get a good look

at B.D.'s wounded shoulder, but the bear moved a few paces away. He said something in Ragayo Spencer didn't understand.

"His Ear-COM, Spencer," Aldo said. "Disconnect."

Spencer hurried to retrieve his mission pack from the hallway where he'd left it. He dug around in the bag, searching for the translating device as he returned to Aldo and B.D. Once he had it, he held it out in his palm, showing it to B.D. The bear lowered his head, tilting it toward Spencer. Spencer fit the device into B.D.'s ear.

"Team," Aldo said as soon as B.D.'s Ear-COM was in place.

"I'm glad to see you two are all right," B.D. said right away.

"We're fine, but are *you* okay?" Spencer tried to look at B.D.'s shoulder. Again, the bear shuffled back a step, moving his left shoulder away.

"I'll be fine. Can you give me an update?"

"I'll update you while Spencer cleans that wound," Aldo said. His tone surprised Spencer. B.D. was the Head of the Guard, but now Aldo was stepping up and taking charge. B.D. glared at the younger bear. His jaw was set in a firm line. Aldo pretended not to notice. "Spencer, what do you have in your mission pack?"

"I have a first aid kit," Spencer answered, looking back and forth between the bears. "And some ginger root."

"I don't need ginger root," B.D. snapped. Spencer could have guessed B.D. wouldn't accept any ginger root, Bearhaven's natural pain killer, in front of him and Aldo. After a moment, B.D. stepped toward Spencer and stretched out on his stomach, giving Spencer full access to his shoulder. "Now, give me the update."

Spencer took one look at B.D.'s shoulder and had to look away. Dora had left her brother with four deep gashes there, and swollen, bloody bite marks down his left leg. B.D. needed stitches. A lot of them. But Spencer didn't have the right tools. His first aid kit would hardly have enough antiseptic to clean all the injuries on B.D.'s huge body. Spencer got to work, furious that Pam, Margo, and Ivan could lock up a badly hurt bear without caring for it first. How did they think they would be able to get their thirty-five thousand dollars for B.D. if he was in too much pain to walk?

Aldo launched into the update. "After we left you and Mark in the parking lot, we hid nearby, but we weren't able to follow you quickly enough to know where you'd been taken."

B.D. flinched as Spencer touched an antiseptic cloth to one of the deeper cuts. Spencer jerked his hand away, afraid to hurt the bear, but B.D. acted as though nothing had happened, so Spencer started to clean the wound again.

"We camped out in one of the old zoo buildings Pam isn't using," Aldo continued. "The Reptile Lodge. And we came to find you this morning. Margo and Ivan towed the Creative Pastry truck . . . So the getaway vehicle is gone. Or at least, it's been moved."

"Are they still here?" B.D. asked. "Margo and Ivan?"

"No," Spencer answered. "We overheard them say they had to leave to catch a flight somewhere as soon as the truck was towed."

"Any leads on where the others are?"

"Not yet," Aldo said.

"And Dora?"

Aldo hesitated. "We haven't seen her since last night."

"Spencer, don't bandage it," B.D. said, turning to Spencer, who was rummaging through the first aid kit. "Thank you," the bear added.

"Are you sure?" Spencer eyed the wound. If he couldn't give B.D. stitches, he should at least bandage the shoulder . . .

"Yes. A bandage will give us away. If Pam or his thugs see it, they'll know I had contact with a human." B.D. explained. "You're going to have to leave me here until the last minute—until we're ready to make our final escape. If you break me out now, they'll know we have more operatives here. It's best if they think we're weak and they've got us all locked up. You will be able to continue to move around Hidden Rock Zoo without the guards on high alert."

"We're just going to leave you in here?" It hadn't occurred to Spencer that they would leave B.D. locked up once they'd found him.

"Yes," B.D. confirmed. "For now."

"All right," Aldo agreed. "Can you direct us from here?"

Spencer's hopes lifted. If they left B.D. with the Ear-COM the Head of the Guard would be able to guide them through the rest of the mission!

"No," B.D. answered right away. "You'll need the Ear-COM."

"What for?" Spencer asked, packing up the first aid kit.

"For Dora," B.D. answered.

Spencer dropped the first aid kit. It clattered loudly to the cement floor. He didn't move to pick it up. He just stared at B.D. in confusion. B.D. was going to send them to Dora, the bear who had nearly torn his leg off and mauled his shoulder less than twenty-four hours earlier?

B.D. looked from Spencer to Aldo. "Why are you looking at me like that?" he asked gruffly.

17

Spencer was starting to worry that the pain was getting to B.D. more than he was letting on. Hadn't the bear learned his lesson? Dora didn't want anything to do with them, and she *definitely* didn't want to be rescued. B.D. had nearly sacrificed the entire mission trying to reason with his violent sister. Now he wanted Spencer and Aldo to go to her again?

"Trust me." B.D.'s voice was firm. "Dora is angry and confused, but she's not crazy. She's obviously still hurt from not making it out of Gutler University during that first rescue and holding everything against me that happened to her since John Shirley and I were rescued, but I don't think she'd hurt you. And she's still our best chance of finding Jane, Shane, and Mark quickly."

Spencer looked at Aldo, hoping the bear would stand up to B.D. again and tell him this plan to send them to Dora was crazy, but Aldo was pacing back and forth by the mouth of B.D's small cave and he didn't say anything.

"How do you know she'll even let us get close enough to talk to her?" Spencer asked, imagining himself putting the Ear-COM in Dora's ear as she huffed and swatted at him with her claws.

"There's something you can say to her . . ." B.D. said slowly. "She'll listen to you if you do."

"What is it?" Spencer asked after a few seconds had passed in silence. Aldo stopped pacing to look at B.D.

"It's something our mother would say to us back, before we were captured," B.D. started. "It translates to 'with you I am home.' Dora, John Shirley, and I would repeat it at Gutler on the worst days to remind ourselves that as long as we were together, protecting one another, we'd be okay. Disconnect," he said so Spencer could hear his Ragayo. Then after a second, *"Yi hu aro valu."*

"Yi hu aro valu," Spencer repeated back.

B.D. nodded. "Team," B.D. reconnected their Ear-COMs. "Say that to Dora. She'll listen to you after you do. And if she still refuses to help, it will at least be enough to protect you."

I hope you're right, Spencer thought, careful not to say it aloud. "Now we just have to find her."

"I already did," Aldo spoke up.

"What?!" Spencer practically shouted. "When?!"

B.D.'s head whipped around to look at Aldo. He winced in pain at his own sudden movement.

"Just now." Aldo padded back to the opening in the cave that led out into the rest of the enclosure. Spencer rushed over to see. When he reached the mouth of the cave, he was sure to keep his body hidden by rock as he peered outside. B.D. limped over to stand behind Aldo.

"Up there."

Spencer followed Aldo's gaze. A hill overlooked the Caves, and perched on top of the hill was Pam's house. The house looked like a modern, high-tech assortment of glass, wood, and iron boxes stacked together, like fancy building blocks. Spencer could see right through some rooms. Others were completely hidden from view. A wooden viewing deck wrapped around the second floor of the house. Spencer could imagine Pam standing there, looking out over his collection of bears in the Caves.

A matching, but much smaller, building stood not far from Pam's house. At first glance, Spencer thought it might be a garage, or a garden shed. But most of the smaller building was made of glass and completely transparent, and after squinting to get a better look at it, Spencer realized there was a bear inside.

Dora was sitting back on her haunches inside the small glass building, staring down at them. Spencer jumped back from the mouth of the cave, but he knew it was too late. Dora had seen him, and by now, she had definitely seen Aldo, too.

18

Spencer closed the door to B.D.'s cave and heard the lock click into place. He glanced through the glass window. B.D. had his back turned. He sat in the mouth of the cave, watching Dora move around her own glass enclosure on the hilltop not far away. Spencer didn't want to leave B.D., but they had no idea when the person who cared for the eight bears in the Caves would arrive, or what Dora might have in mind for Spencer and Aldo now that she knew they were still moving around the property. Spencer and Aldo needed to get out of the Caves while they still could.

"Did you find any food?" Spencer called down the hall to Aldo, who was beside the polar bear enclosure, rummaging around the supply shelves lining the wall.

"It's hard to say," Aldo answered. He sniffed at a row of large bags on the bottom shelf. "This smells a little bit like food . . ." Spencer walked over to Aldo. He crouched down to examine one of the bags Aldo was nosing into. *Bear Kibble* it read. Spencer pulled a half-full bag toward himself. He unfolded the top and looked inside.

"You can eat this," he said, grabbing a handful of kibble

from the bag. It looked like oversized dog food. Aldo lowered his snout to the kibble in Spencer's hand.

"You're sure?" The bear didn't seem very impressed by the smell.

"I'm sure." Spencer dropped the handful of kibble back into its bag and pushed it toward Aldo. "It's not exactly a dinner at Raymond's, but eat as much as you can, just in case we don't find anything better and can't get back here for a while."

Aldo didn't seem to need any more encouragement to eat. He buried his head in the bag and started to crunch. Spencer stood up and scanned the rest of the supplies. Hopefully, he wouldn't have to eat bear kibble himself, but at least they knew it was here if he got desperate.

As Aldo gulped down the bear kibble, Spencer reviewed the plan that he, B.D., and Aldo had worked out back in B.D.'s cave cell. They were going to make their way to the grove of trees near Dora's enclosure, and find a hiding place that gave them a view of B.D. The Head of the Guard would watch Pam in his house overlooking the Caves. When Pam went to bed, B.D. would rise onto his hind legs, signaling to Aldo and Spencer that the coast was clear.

Aldo removed his head from the empty bag. "I guess that was better than nothing," he said, snorting kibble crumbs out of his nose.

"Ready to go?" Spencer grabbed the bag and crumpled it up. He shoved it to the back of the shelf.

"Ready." Aldo led the way to the door. He smelled the bottom edge of the door, then stepped aside for Spencer to open it. Spencer peeked out into the shadowed alleyway. Nobody was there. They quietly stepped outside. "Climb on." Aldo immediately crouched low enough for Spencer to swing onto his back.

When Spencer had a good hold on Aldo, the bear padded toward the opening at the end of the alley and beyond the protection of the rock formation. He stayed close to the wall as they took a closer look at the route they'd planned.

In order to get to the grove on the hilltop beside Pam's home and Dora's matching enclosure, Spencer and Aldo would have to cross the lawn between the Airy Aviary and the Caves, then make their way up the neatly gardened hill. The open space would be dangerous, particularly because they didn't know exactly where Pam was. They hadn't seen him since last night. There was no telling when he might step out onto his viewing deck, or drive up to his own front door, returning from wherever it was Pam spent his time.

"I don't know about this, Aldo," Spencer whispered. "It feels too risky to move now, when we don't know where exactly Pam is."

"I feel the same way. But we can't stay here. Sooner or later, someone's going to come feed the bears. It's better for us to move now, when no one has any reason to be paying attention to the Caves." Without waiting for Spencer's reply, Aldo lurched forward, making a break for the hill and the grove.

Spencer could feel Aldo hurtling over flower beds, trying to leave as little evidence as possible of their sprint through Pam's neat garden. He held on tightly to the bear, his body leaned low against Aldo's back, and soon enough, they were leaving the ground, climbing up into the limbs of a tree.

"Ouch!" Spencer whispered. Something knocked him in the head as they moved around the branches. *Ouch!* He got clocked in the head again. *What* was *that?* Spencer didn't lift his head to look until Aldo had stopped moving.

"I think our luck has officially changed," Aldo said quietly. Spencer peeled himself off Aldo, looking around the tree for the first time.

Pears!

The tree was full of pears! The leafy branches were bursting with them. Spencer scrambled off Aldo's back, carefully finding his own branch in the tree to perch on. Finally, something Spencer could eat!

"And I've got a view of B.D.," Aldo added.

Spencer didn't answer. He was too busy pulling his first pear off the tree. His stomach growled. He didn't care that the leaves around the pear rustled. He took a big bite of the pear, then heard Pam's voice.

"Can I *help* you with something?"

Spencer froze. Fruit juice dripped down his chin.

Aldo's eyes widened. "I may have spoken too soon about our luck changing . . ." the bear grunted quietly.

"I said, can I help you?" Pam's high-pitched voice carried up into the thick, leafy branches of the pear tree from somewhere Spencer couldn't see.

Spencer started to panic. *What are we going to do?!* But then another voice reached them.

"I apologize . . . sir. I'm your . . . your manicurist for the day," the woman's voice stammered. "Your assistant called to schedule—" Spencer clapped a hand over his mouth and almost gagged. *She has to touch Pam's fingernails!*

"Where's Tobias?" Pam asked. "Tobias knows how I like them done."

"He wasn't able—"

"Fine. All right. Come in."

Spencer and Aldo didn't relax until they were sure Pam and his manicurist had gone inside Pam's house.

"I thought the mission was ruined," Spencer whispered, taking a big bite of pear.

"So did I," Aldo answered. "But Pam didn't see us. It's not over yet."

19

"Aldo," Spencer whispered, taking his eyes off B.D. for the first time in what felt like hours. The moon was high above the Caves, casting just enough light into B.D.'s enclosure for Spencer to see the bear. He hadn't moved from the mouth of his cave since Spencer and Aldo had left him. Even when the zookeeper had come to clean the space and leave food for B.D., the bear had stayed put, swatting the ground angrily anytime the worker got too close.

Aldo stirred on the branch beside Spencer. They had stayed in the tree and taken turns standing guard all afternoon and evening. During his last shift, Spencer had heard the manicurist say good-bye to Pam and let herself out, and then he saw Pam and Dora leave together soon after. They had returned an hour later, during Aldo's shift, while Spencer rested. Now, after hours of keeping watch from the tree, finally, B.D. was rising onto his hind legs in his own enclosure, giving the signal Spencer had been waiting for.

"Time to go?" Aldo asked. His ears and snout twitched, gathering information.

"Yes. Look," Spencer pushed a leafy branch aside, clearing a space for Aldo to see B.D., who stood unsteadily on his hind legs. Spencer pulled the flashlight out of his mission pack and aimed it toward B.D. in the Caves. He turned it on, then off again quickly, signaling to B.D. they had received his message—Pam had gone to bed. The coast was clear for Spencer and Aldo to go to Dora. B.D. dropped back to all fours.

Aldo climbed down from the pear tree without wasting a second, but Spencer hesitated. The last time they were close to Dora, she was viciously attacking B.D. He wasn't exactly eager to see her again, but according to this plan, the sooner he did, the sooner he would see Mom and Dad.

Spencer carefully climbed out of the tree. Once he joined Aldo on the ground, they crept out of the grove toward Dora's enclosure. As they got closer, Spencer realized *enclosure* wasn't the right word for Dora's home.

Glass sliding doors made up an entire wall of the small building, and now those doors stood open. Dora could come and go as she pleased. The rest of the structure seemed to be an imitation of Pam's own large home. Parts of the small square building were hidden from view with wood and iron walls, and portions of the glass walls were covered by enormous velvety gray curtains, but most of Dora's home was completely transparent. Dora padded into view. She bowed her head to drink from a crystal clear stream that ran through the middle of her home.

Spencer and Aldo stepped onto the path that led straight through the open glass doors to Dora. *Here we go,* Spencer thought. He knew how important it was for this meeting to go well. If Dora attacked them, the mission would be over, and his chances of rescuing everyone would be gone.

Dora lifted her head from the stream. Her ears flicked in the direction of the open doors. Aldo didn't stop walking. Dora huffed and rose onto her hind legs, facing the door.

Spencer cast an anxious glance down at the Caves. He could tell that B.D. was watching them, but if things didn't go well between Dora, Spencer, and Aldo, then B.D., locked in his cave, wouldn't be able to help. Spencer hoped that his teammates knew what they were doing, sending them here to walk right into Dora's home with no protection and zero backup . . .

Pop! Dora's warning stopped Spencer in his tracks. Aldo kept walking.

"Maruh," Aldo growled to Dora, as "hello" translated through Spencer's Ear-COM. Dora didn't answer. Her eyes flicked back and forth between Aldo and Spencer. *"Maruh, anbranda,"* Aldo said, adding the bears' word for "friend" to his greeting. He continued to approach Dora.

Spencer waited for Dora to warn them with the jaw-popping sound again. When she didn't, he took a step forward, falling in behind Aldo on the path. Dora huffed, but Aldo didn't stop when he reached the open glass doors. He crossed the threshold into Dora's home. Spencer wished he could reach for his jade bear now, to muster some courage. *I just have to be brave enough without it,* he told himself firmly and stepped inside after Aldo. Dora huffed again.

"We're coming to you as friends, Dora. We are here to help you, and we need your help," Aldo said. "We only mean—"

Dora dropped to all fours and cut Aldo off with a jaw pop. She stepped toward him, showing her teeth.

"Aldo," Spencer said. "Maybe this isn't such—"

Dora's eyes flicked to Spencer. *Pop!* She stepped forward and thrust her face into his.

"Yi hu aro valu," Spencer blurted out the phrase B.D. had taught them. Dora froze. *"Yi hu aro valu,"* Spencer repeated, his growls coming out as gasps.

Dora looked at Aldo. She dropped back a few paces, moving away from Spencer.

"With you I am home," Aldo said. "B.D. asked us to relay that message to you. He hoped it would show you we are friends of your family. We just need to talk to you. We have something that can help us all communicate. It's safe—I'm wearing one in my ear now. If you're willing, Spencer can give you one."

Dora's head was bowed, but she seemed to be listening. She growled back at Aldo, but Spencer couldn't understand her. Dora swung her head in Spencer's direction, grunting, then began to pace the length of her indoor stream.

"Yes, he is a Plain, and he's loyal to bears. You can trust him," Aldo growled. A moment later, Dora turned and charged at Spencer.

"Aldo!" Spencer hissed. He put both hands up to hold off the bear, but it was too late, Dora had reached him. She headbutted him in the stomach with another grunt.

"She wants the Ear-COM," Aldo said, stepping closer as though to protect Spencer if Dora changed her mind.

20

Spencer's hands shook as he fit the translating device into Dora's ear. As soon as it was in place, he stepped back.

"Team," Aldo said, connecting his own Ear-COM with Dora's and Spencer's. Dora winced, then shook her head as though trying to shake a fly off her fur. "Dora, can you hear me?"

"I can hear you better than I want to," Dora answered.

"Uh . . . it's nice to meet you, Dora," Spencer said awkwardly. He forced a smile. Dora shot him a blank stare, then turned her back on Spencer and Aldo. She walked a lap around the inside of her home before speaking again. She passed each of the four big, perfect trees in the four corners of the square building, circling the stream that made a soothing, babbling sound as it ran through the middle of the room. The section of the building hidden from the outdoors by a wood-and-iron wall and gray curtains was outfitted similarly to the bears' cave-like bedrooms in Bearhaven. It was the only part of Dora's home that was covered by a roof. *She must sleep there.*

"All of this is mine," Dora said at last. "My home. Do you know how I used to live?"

Spencer gulped. This wasn't how he'd imagined the conversation going, but Dora had taken charge.

"I used to live in a tiny cage with my brothers at Gutler University. You see my muzzle? You see no fur here?" Dora thrust her head into their faces, showing them the furless patch of skin on her jaw. It matched the one on B.D.'s own muzzle. "Margo always put the food outside the bars of our cage. We had to push our jaws through the bars to eat. Every bite hurt but we were starving. It was a bad life but at least we were together. Then your family came and took my family away. But not me." She glared at Spencer. "And my *family* left me. You think a bear can survive like that? Starved and hurt all the time with nobody to trust? No. Did that matter to your family, or mine? No. Nobody came back for me."

Spencer opened his mouth to explain. Mom and Dad *had* gone back for Dora, but they were too late. Dora had already disappeared from Gutler. Dora bared her teeth at Spencer, and he closed his mouth.

"Pam took me from Margo and Ivan, and now I live here and have all the food I want without any help from my family *or* yours," Dora went on bitterly. "You came here thinking I needed you to rescue me? Ha! Now look where you are. I am free here, and you are trapped. You all need *me* to save *you*. But why should I help you? I don't need any of you, just like none of you—*none* of you—needed me all these years." Dora sat back on her haunches in front of Spencer and Aldo, glaring at them both.

Spencer didn't know what to say. He understood why Dora was so angry. She had spent twelve years thinking she had been abandoned by her family and forgotten by humans she had once trusted.

"Dora," Aldo started, "B.D. has never recovered from losing you that night at Gutler, and neither have the Plains." The bear's voice was calm; he sounded more like his father, Professor Weaver, than he ever had before. "They have all been looking for you on every single rescue mission. They built Bearhaven, and every day they wished you were there. They have saved over one hundred bears, and every single time, on every single rescue mission, they hoped the next bear they'd save would be you."

"How would you know that?" Dora snapped. "You two are just cubs. You can't possibly know how I feel."

Aldo hesitated.

"I know how you feel," Spencer spoke up.

Dora narrowed her eyes at him.

"I know because my family was taken away from me, too. And I know what it feels like to be the one who's safe. It doesn't feel . . . better. I'm missing a big piece of my life, too. I won't ever stop trying to get my parents back. And I know you don't like my parents right now, but they did try to rescue you again. You weren't at Gutler anymore, and they couldn't find you. B.D. really does look for you every time he leaves Bearhaven. And even at Bearhaven—"

"Quiet," Dora cut Spencer off. He thought she was just tired of listening to him speak, but then he saw Aldo's ears twitch.

"Pam?" Aldo asked, his eyes locked on Dora. Spencer strained to hear what the bears were hearing.

"Yes." Dora sat back on her haunches. Spencer couldn't

read her expression. "He's coming. If you try to leave now he'll see you," she added. Her voice was flat, like she didn't care what happened to Spencer and Aldo next.

"We're trapped . . ." Spencer whispered.

"Hide," Aldo ordered.

Spencer sprang into action. He sprinted into the darkest corner of Dora's home and pushed the heavy gray curtain aside, stepping in behind it. He was careful to fit his body into one of the folds.

"You're safe there, Spencer," Aldo said, confirming Spencer was hidden from view.

"What about you?" Spencer asked.

"Tree," Aldo said after a second. Then the Ear-COMs fell silent.

Spencer tried to take a few deep breaths, but the air caught in his throat. Had they gotten through to Dora? Would she cover for them? Spencer didn't know, but they were at Dora's mercy now. It wouldn't take much for her to give Spencer and Aldo away to Pam.

Spencer heard footsteps on the path just outside.

"Good evening, Dora."

He's here.

21

"How are you tonight, my Dora?" Pam said. Spencer hated the sound of Pam's voice. It was singsongy and sweet, but Spencer wasn't fooled. He'd heard Pam say threatening and evil words in that very same voice. And why wasn't Pam in bed? Had B.D. gotten the signal wrong? "Keeping an eye on your brother?" Pam went on. "Don't worry, he'll be gone before you know it."

The room fell silent. Spencer couldn't see anything from behind the curtain, but he guessed Pam was stroking Dora's head with his gross, long fingernails, the same way he had at the auction the night before.

The Ear-COM! Suddenly, Spencer's mind was racing. *What if Pam sees it?!* The tiny piece of gear tucked in Dora's ear was enough to put the entire mission at risk if Pam spotted it! Spencer's stomach twisted. How could he have forgotten about the Ear-COM when he rushed to hide?!

"Of course, he has to heal before I can ship him off, thanks to your little temper tantrum, my dear." Pam interrupted Spencer's thoughts. "I sold him for thousands of dollars. I can't deliver him damaged, now can I?"

Spencer clenched his jaw. How could Pam talk about

B.D. that way? Spencer wished the Ear-COM worked the same way as the BEAR-COM. If the device was going to put the whole mission at risk, Dora should at least be able to hear the terrible things Pam was saying, but Spencer knew the technology didn't work that way. It only translated back and forth between other connected devices. Dora couldn't understand what Pam was saying now.

"You, Dora, would sell for much more than your brother, though, wouldn't you? You are so much smarter—and such a beautiful bear. Those dealers would have spent *tens and tens* of thousands on you. But you're worth more to me. I won't sell you, Dora. Not for a long time anyway." The room fell silent again. Spencer gritted his teeth. *Please don't give us away, Dora!* he thought. All she would have to do was sniff once in Spencer's direction, and Pam could be on to him.

"Well," Pam said after a few more seconds, "I came because I forgot to close you in for the night. I don't know why you insist on visiting our friends after I go to sleep. But I don't like it, so it ends tonight." Footsteps sounded through the room. "Good night, Dora."

Spencer listened to the sound of doors sliding shut. He waited for Dora or Aldo to give him some sign it was safe to come out of hiding. After a few minutes, Dora spoke up.

"He's gone."

Spencer stepped out from behind the curtain. Out of the corner of his eye, he saw Aldo climbing down from his hiding spot in one of Dora's four trees. The glass doors had been closed and latched on the outside.

"We're locked in?" Spencer could hear the nerves in his own voice.

"You think after all these years I haven't figured out how to get in and out of here when I want to?" Dora asked bluntly.

"Oh . . . right."

"Does he always lock you in at night?" Aldo asked, padding over to Dora and Spencer.

"No."

"He said it was because you've been visiting someone," Spencer said. "Pam doesn't like it." *Wait* . . . Suddenly, Spencer was bursting with questions. He blurted them out. "Is it my parents? And Uncle Mark? Who you've been visiting? Can you tell us where they are, Dora? Please?"

Dora looked away. "Tell me what else he said."

Spencer hesitated, afraid telling Dora what Pam had said would make her angry again.

"What did he say?" the bear repeated.

"He said that B.D. will only be here until the wounds you gave him heal. Then, Pam said, he's going to send B.D. to the animal dealer he sold him to last night," Spencer started.

"What does that mean, Spencer?" Aldo stared at Spencer in confusion.

Spencer looked back and forth between Aldo and Dora. There was no sense holding back the truth now. "Last night, Pam sold some Bearhaven bears in an auction. B.D. was one of those bears."

"But . . . he didn't know he'd have B.D.," Aldo said. "Why would he—"

"What else did Pam say?" Dora interrupted impatiently.

"He said he could sell you for a lot more than what he

sold B.D. for," Spencer watched Dora closely. Her eyes clouded with anger. "But he doesn't want to sell you," Spencer rushed to add. "He's not going to. Yet. Then he said he was closing you in tonight because he didn't like you visiting someone. That's it. I swear." Spencer held his breath, waiting for Dora to react. When she didn't, he decided to try asking her about Mom, Dad, and Uncle Mark again. "Dora, do you know where Pam is keeping my family?"

Dora stared blankly back at Spencer. Aldo's head was bowed low. He looked lost in thought, like he was still trying to make sense of the fact that Pam had sold Bearhaven bears.

"Dora, please—" Spencer was getting desperate.

"Yes," she cut him off. "I know where your parents are."

"Will you tell us?"

"Why should I?" Dora challenged him.

"Because if you tell Aldo and me where to find them, we can rescue them. Then all of us, *including* you and B.D., can get out of Hidden Rock Zoo. You will never have to worry about being locked in anywhere ever again, and you'll never have to worry about Pam selling you. Ever." Spencer tried to sound confident.

Dora started to pace. "I've trusted the Plains before, and that didn't go well for me."

"Give us another chance. Please, Dora," Spencer pleaded. "We could both be reunited with our families."

Dora padded over to the gray curtain. She sat back on her haunches and pushed it aside, revealing Pam's house looming over her own. "You will have to earn it," she said.

"Earn what?" Spencer asked.

"Another chance for the Plains. My trust. The information you want. All of it." Dora let the curtain fall back into place. She turned around. "I'll make a deal with you."

A deal? Spencer and Aldo exchanged a look. That did not sound good.

22

"This isn't going to be easy," Dora said.

Spencer nodded. He hadn't expected whatever deal Dora was willing to make to be easy. But he would do whatever it took to find out where in Hidden Rock Zoo his family was being held prisoner.

"I have a cub," Dora started. "Darwin. He's three months old, but I haven't been allowed contact with him since the day he was born. Pam took him away. Now Darwin lives in Pam's house with a special caretaker who stays with him during the day. He's treated like a pet or a prince—but I am his mother. My cub should be with me." Dora paused.

Spencer tried to make sense of what she was saying, but before he could understand why Pam would want to separate a cub from its mother, or what any of this had to do with him and Aldo and the information they needed for the mission, Dora spoke again. "I want you to bring him to me. Tonight."

Spencer's jaw dropped open. Aldo shifted uneasily on all fours. They both stared back at Dora in disbelief. She was asking them to risk everything. He looked at the glass doors Pam had closed when he left. Part of Spencer wished Dora *didn't* know how to get out of here. Dora broke the silence.

"If you do this for me, I'll give you the information you want. I'll know I can trust you," Dora said. "I'll believe you're not just here for yourselves, and you can convince me my family really does mean something to you. Darwin is B.D.'s nephew. If B.D. is as loyal to his family as you believe, he would never leave my cub behind. And if you understand what it feels like to be separated from your family like you say, you won't let our family continue to suffer apart from one another."

Spencer gulped. "So let me get this straight . . . your cub, Darwin, is in Pam's house. And we have to . . . bring him to you . . . tonight."

"In exchange for information about your family. Yes," Dora confirmed.

"Why does Pam keep Darwin in his house instead of with you? Or in the Caves with the other bears?" Aldo asked.

"Pam is raising my cub himself for something special. I don't know what he has planned, but Darwin is not just any black bear."

Spencer watched Dora closely, but she didn't go on. *I guess I'll have to find out for myself what that means*, he thought. "Do you know where exactly he is kept in Pam's house?" Spencer asked. He crossed his fingers, hoping Darwin was kept as far from Pam's bedroom as possible.

Dora nodded. "In a special room off Pam's private office on the second floor."

The second floor? "What floor is Pam's bedroom on?"

"The second floor," Dora said, and for the first time, Spencer thought she sounded a little apologetic. "His bedroom is next to his office."

"Dora." Aldo sounded concerned. "Do you think it's even possible for us to get Darwin without Pam finding out?"

Dora was silent for a moment. "It's possible," she said at last. "It's risky. But it is possible. I wouldn't suggest it if it wasn't. But the Plain will have to go in alone. If a bear could do it, I would have done it myself long ago."

"Spencer," Spencer whispered, his mouth suddenly dry. "My name is Spencer."

Dora nodded. "Spencer, if you bring me my cub tonight, I'll tell you where to find your family. I will do what I can to help you."

"Okay," Spencer said. He looked at Aldo. "I'll do it."

"I wish I could go with you," Aldo said. The bear looked as scared as Spencer felt. "But I'll be with you through the Ear-COM the whole time."

"I know," Spencer answered. He turned to Dora. "How do I get out of here?"

Dora looked up. Spencer followed her gaze.

"This just gets better and better," he muttered. Dora's home didn't have a roof, and the tops of the trees had grown above the glass walls. They reached up into the sky, their branches arching outward. A tree just outside Dora's home loomed in the night. Its branches curved over the glass wall. The branches reached into Dora's home, and intersecting with Dora's tallest tree, created a tangled bridge of branches over the glass.

23

Spencer climbed up into the limbs of the tallest tree in Dora's home. The farther he got from the ground, the more he wished he was on Aldo's back, and that Aldo was with him for this cub-napping mission. Spencer was confident Aldo would never fall from a tree. Spencer on the other hand . . . he hated climbing. But just before he could be gripped by the terrible sensation of blood and falling through leaves and branches that usually overcame him when he climbed, he caught sight of something familiar in the crook of the branch above him. It reflected the moonlight. He climbed toward it.

When Spencer reached the scrap of green-and-gold-sequined fabric he had seen from below he stopped to take a closer look. The fabric was tucked into a knothole in the tree, as though Dora had put it there for safekeeping. Spencer recognized the cloth, and he knew exactly where the fabric had come from. It matched the flag that flew in Bearhaven in Dora's honor. He had been told by B.D. himself that it was a scrap of the sequined uniform the Benally siblings had been made to wear as mascots at Gutler University. And that it was flown as a flag to commemorate the original rescue and . . .

Dora. Deeper in the knothole, Spencer also spotted a tuft of golden-white fur.

"Spencer? Is everything okay?" It was Aldo, watching from the ground below. His and Spencer's Ear-COMs were still connected.

"Yeah, almost at the top." Spencer got back to climbing. When he reached the highest branch that still looked strong enough to hold his weight, he stopped climbing and squinted, trying to make out which branches belonged to the tree he was in now, and which ones belonged to the tree rooted in the ground outside.

"Okay," Spencer whispered, eyeing a sturdy looking branch that he could see led to the tree trunk a few yards beyond the glass wall. Dora was probably almost two hundred pounds heavier than Spencer. If the branch could hold her weight, and she could escape this way, it would be able to hold Spencer. "I can do this," he said aloud.

"You can do this," Aldo repeated through the Ear-COM.

Spencer crouched down. He wrapped his arms and legs around the branch that formed a bridge across the gap between the tree inside Dora's home, and the one outside it. The bark scraped against him as he scooted across the branch on his belly, but Spencer barely noticed. He was so focused on not losing his grip and falling that nothing else mattered. Before long, Spencer was surrounded by the thick branches of the tree that extended outside Dora's home. He climbed through those branches until he reached the tree's lowest limbs and jumped to the ground from there, landing with a soft thud. He was outside, beyond the walls of Dora's house.

Spencer glanced back through the glass wall. Dora and Aldo were watching him. He nodded, then crept into the dark toward Pam's looming house. Dora had explained that since the security surrounding Hidden Rock Zoo was so tight the interior of the zoo didn't need much additional security. Nobody was ever permitted to enter who didn't work for Pam, and the only way into the property was through the front gates. Pam was so confident no one would be able to get through the outside walls of Hidden Rock Zoo, he didn't even lock the door to his house. She'd said it as though it should make Spencer feel better about what he had to do. It didn't.

"Front path," Spencer whispered, updating Aldo on his location as he snuck up the white stone path that led to Pam's front door. Spencer put his hand on the iron knob of the wooden door. "I'm going in," he whispered as quietly as he possibly could. Spencer would have to use his best Bear Stealth operative training to move through the house soundlessly. He wouldn't be able to speak once he was inside, so he didn't expect to be able to update Aldo again.

"Good luck," Aldo said.

Slowly, Spencer pushed the door open just enough to slip inside. He didn't close it behind himself when he stepped into the black marble foyer but left the door open, afraid to make one more tiny sound than he had to. He tried to make out his surroundings in the strange house barely lit by the moon but couldn't really see anything.

Spencer crouched down and carefully took off his mission pack. He unzipped it without a sound and pulled out the night-vision goggles. The slingshot slipped out of his bag and clattered noisily to the black marble floor.

No! Spencer tried hard not to gasp, panicking. He was totally motionless, all his muscles tense and ready to run if he had to. But nothing happened. The house was still quiet, or quiet except for the sound of rushing water. Spencer picked up the slingshot and slipped it back into his bag, then pulled the night-vision goggles on over his eyes. Through the special lenses, he could finally see the house around him.

He stood up from the floor of the large entryway. To his right was a living room. Its floor was completely covered in bearskin rugs. Spencer thought there must be dozens of them, laid out side by side throughout the entire room. He was glad to look away. To his left, a wide doorway led to a dining room with a long, dark table in the center. And straight ahead there was a big winding staircase leading upstairs.

"So far so good?" Aldo's voice rang in Spencer's ear, making him jump. "Stay silent if the answer is yes."

Spencer was silent. Sticking close to the wall, he stepped on the first stair, setting his foot down evenly and putting his weight on it slowly. He strained his ears, listening for the tiniest creak of wood. Nothing came. Spencer's silent walking was working. All that Bear Stealth training he had done with Kate and Aldo back in Bearhaven was paying off! He climbed the stairs in complete silence, focusing all his attention on each glowing green step.

When Spencer stepped off the top stair of the staircase and onto the second-floor landing, he heard a loud, wheezing snore. *Pam!*

24

Spencer crept down a long hallway toward the snores. Dora said Pam's office was next to Pam's bedroom, so Spencer was sure he was on the right track. He crept to the last door in the hall and was relieved to see it was Pam's office. He spotted the door to Darwin's room right away and silent-walked over to it, pulling off his night-vision goggles as he went. He didn't want to scare the cub. Spencer opened the door and felt around on the wall inside the room until he found a light switch.

"A light just went on in the house," Spencer heard Aldo report in his ear.

"It's me," he whispered back, closing the door behind him. He resisted telling Aldo how cool Darwin's room was. Part of it had been made to look like a forest. Miniature trees took up half the space. Spencer walked over to them, searching the branches. He knew cubs liked to flop their limbs over tree branches and sleep, but he didn't see Darwin anywhere. Before turning away from the little cluster of trees, Spencer reached out to touch the trunk of one. *It's fake!* he thought, impressed by how real the artificial bark looked.

On the far side of the room, Spencer spotted a little cave.

Spencer quietly approached it. When he was only a few steps away, a little paw poked out of the mouth of the cave, stretching straight out. Then another paw joined it. Spencer stepped closer. In the dark cave, he could just make out the rest of the cub's slumbering body.

Spencer crouched down. *"Maruh,"* he quietly growled a hello.

The paws disappeared, quickly drawn back into the dark bundle of fur. Darwin scrambled clumsily to all fours and tripped over his paws, flopping deeper into the cave to hide.

"Shala." Spencer whispered the Ragayo word for "safe."

A second later, Darwin poked his head out of the artificial cave. His fur was jet-black, like Dora's, but even darker somehow. The way the cub's black fur gleamed reminded Spencer of the black jade of his bear figurine. Darwin blinked at Spencer, the big ears the cub hadn't grown into yet twitched. His little black nose sniffed nervously. Spencer was careful to stay completely still as he watched the cub.

Darwin seemed to gain some confidence. He took a few cautious steps forward, until his whole body was framed in the mouth of the cave. Spencer caught a glimpse of white fur on the cub's chest. *A blaze mark!* Spencer smiled, hoping for a better look at the cub's marking. Just then, Darwin's curious snout seemed to get the best of him. The cub wobbled up onto his hind legs. He nose sniffed rapidly in Spencer's direction.

At the sight of Darwin's blaze mark, Spencer gasped.

Darwin dropped back to all fours, frightened.

"I'm sorry," Spencer whispered, his eyes wide and locked on the shining fur in the middle of Darwin's jet-black chest. The blaze mark was in the perfect shape of a crown. Spencer

had never seen anything like it. Usually, blaze marks were swoops or blotches of white fur. Professor Weaver had a triangular blaze mark, but still . . . that was nothing like the perfect crown symbol that seemed emblazoned on Darwin's chest in shining silver fur. The rest of Darwin's fur was so dark that the crown practically glowed.

How had Pam managed it? Spencer wondered. He knew Pam had scientists who had already done crazy things with bears. After all, there was the microchipping technology that Pam used on the whole bear army. But this was different. Spencer knew that bears were born with their blaze marks. Somehow, Darwin had been born with Pam's symbol of his power, the crown, on his chest.

Spencer looked up at the cub's face. Darwin was peering out of the cave anxiously. "I wonder what else is special about you," Spencer whispered, knowing there must be more. Darwin shrunk back even farther, and Spencer pushed the question out of his head. Now wasn't the time to solve the mystery of Pam's prized cub.

Spencer wasn't sure if the cub understood his Ragayo, but he hoped the tone of his voice would communicate that he wasn't going to hurt Darwin. *"Shala,"* he said. Darwin poked his head back out.

Darwin padded closer, sniffing first at the mission pack on the ground, then at the coil of rope, then finally at Spencer himself. Spencer tried not to laugh as Darwin's snout tickled his shin. "Now I just have to get you to ride quietly in this sling I made for you," Spencer whispered to the cub. *"Shala, anbranda,"* he added as he reached out to touch Darwin.

"Wow," Spencer whispered, petting Darwin. The cub's fur was softer than anything Spencer had ever felt before. Kate's fur was soft, like a fluffy dog, but Darwin's was somehow softer still. Spencer retrieved the little knob of ginger root from his mission pack, then returned the backpack to his back.

"Here goes nothing." He placed the ginger root on the floor between himself and Darwin. Darwin lowered his snout to sniff at it. He extended a shiny black claw and jabbed the root, then picked it up with his mouth. Adrenaline started to pump into Spencer's veins. He knew how loud cubs could be when they were in distress. There would be no hiding the sound. As Darwin started to gnaw the ginger root, Spencer reached forward and picked the cub up in his arms. He was relieved by how light Darwin was. He couldn't be more than ten pounds, and the rope sling would definitely be secure enough to hold him.

"You're going to come with me, *anbranda*," Spencer cooed as quietly as he could. "So far so good. *Shala.*" Darwin continued to gnaw the ginger root, allowing Spencer to tuck him into the rope sling he'd made. "Look how comfortable you are. You're just going for a fun ride." Spencer couldn't believe his luck. Darwin was so captivated by the ginger root, he hadn't protested being carried at all, but Spencer didn't know how long that would last.

Spencer got to his feet. He grabbed his night-vision goggles from the ground where he'd left them and tugged them on over his eyes. He strode quickly to the door, snapped off the light, and let himself and Darwin out into

Pam's office. Spencer paused, waiting for the sound of Pam's snore. The moment he heard it, he made a break for it, running as fast and as quietly as he could, holding Darwin against him in the knotted sling. Silently, with Spencer landing lightly with every stride, they flew through the hall, down the stairs, and out Pam's front door.

25

"I got him!" Spencer gave a hushed cheer into his Ear-COM as he climbed the tree to return to Dora and Aldo. Darwin started to make a light humming sound in his rope sling, but he didn't sound afraid, and Spencer knew that in minutes, he would be reuniting the cub with his mother. Spencer reached the branch that extended out over the glass wall surrounding Dora's home and overlapped with the tree inside the enclosure. After checking to make sure the cub was secure, and each of the knots would hold, he crawled out across the branch.

"Great work, little man," Aldo replied through the Ear-COM.

Spencer climbed down through the branches of the tree inside Dora's home. This time, when he passed the knothole where Dora had stored a scrap of her Gutler uniform, he recognized the tuft of silver-colored fur. It was probably all Dora had of Darwin . . . until now.

Dora was up on her hind legs at the base of the tree. Her front paws were firmly planted on the trunk, and her eyes were glued to Spencer as he descended toward her. As soon as he dropped to the ground, he untangled Darwin from the rope sling and set him in front of Dora, who immediately began to nuzzle her cub. Darwin scrambled to all fours, burrowing into his mother's fur, making a sound like a helicopter that Spencer knew showed the cub's happiness.

A lump rose in Spencer's throat, and he had to look away. He didn't want to interrupt Dora and Darwin's reunion, but he was desperate for it to be his turn to see his mom, and the rest of his own family. How long would he have to wait before Dora turned over the information she'd promised?

Spencer left Dora and Darwin together, and joined Aldo, who had settled himself beside the stream.

"That blaze mark," Aldo said, his eyes on Darwin. "I've never seen one like it."

"I know," Spencer answered. He pulled off the night-vision goggles—out here, the moonlight was enough to see—and started to untie the network of knots he had used to harness Darwin to his chest.

"I hadn't either, and I don't think it's a concidence that it matches Pam's crown logo. I wonder what else Pam has done to make him special."

"I'm sure we'll find out soon enough. How was it in there?" Aldo jerked his muzzle in the direction of Pam's home.

"Creepy." Spencer thought back to the living room with its dozens of bearskin rugs. "And Pam snores. But it was worth the risk to go in there. At least we're one step closer to finding Mom, Dad, and Uncle Mark."

Aldo avoided Spencer's eyes. The bear bowed his head and drank from the stream.

"What's the matter? We are one step closer . . . right?"

Aldo lifted his head and looked at Dora and Darwin. The cub was clambering onto his mother's back. "It's just . . ."

Spencer's stomach flopped. He had no idea what Aldo was about to say, but he couldn't stand to hear they weren't really going to find Mom and Dad in a matter of minutes.

"As soon as Pam wakes up and realizes Darwin is gone, he's going to lock down all of Hidden Rock Zoo," Aldo explained. "That cub is obviously his most prized possession."

"But . . . what about . . . we have to . . ." Spencer stammered, but he knew Aldo was right. What were they going to do? Dora had tricked him!

"I know. I thought we were going to go find your parents and Mark right away, but if we can't be sure we'll be able to make all four of our rescues—Jane and Shane and Mark and B.D.—before Pam wakes up, getting out of Hidden Rock Zoo is going to be a whole lot harder. And we both know it was never going to be easy to begin with. The last thing we need is for Pam to put all the Hidden Rock Zoo guards on high alert." Aldo watched the mother bear snuggle with her cub. "I don't know if this was a trick . . . or if Dora just hasn't realized yet. But we—you—are going to have to put the cub back where you found him. And it's been a long night already, I don't think you should wait too long to do it."

"No," Spencer groaned. He stopped untying knots and let the rope hang over his shoulders. *It's not fair!* He'd brought Dora her cub; now she needed to tell them where to find Mom, Dad, and Uncle Mark. That was the deal! Going back into Pam's office now to return Darwin to his special room meant even more delay, and even more risk. "Disconnect," he said, frustrated. "Team," he connected his Ear-COM with

Dora and Aldo's. He knew how much Dora's time with Darwin must mean to both bears, but soon enough they'd be together in Bearhaven. Right now Spencer had to get the mission back on track.

"Dora, where is my family being held?" he asked right away. The mother bear didn't so much as flick an ear in Spencer's direction. "Dora, you promised."

Dora lifted her head. Darwin nipped at her ear. "They're in the aquarium." She said offhandedly, her attention still focused on Darwin.

"The aquarium?" Spencer looked at Aldo. "There wasn't an aquarium on the map."

"What map?" Dora asked.

"We have an old zoo map, from when Hidden Rock Zoo first opened, and there *definitely* is not an aquarium on it." Spencer reached for his map. Was Dora really tricking them?

"It wouldn't be on the map. It was never finished," Dora explained as Darwin slipped off her back. "It was supposed to be unveiled later."

"Where is it?" Spencer's heart started to pound. This was it! He was really going to find Mom and Dad at last!

"There's an entrance beyond the Airy Aviary," Dora said, pausing to pick Darwin up off the ground and set him back on his paws. "It doesn't look like much, but you'll find it."

Spencer could barely stand his excitement. "Aldo, let's go." The bear didn't budge. "Come on," Spencer started, impatiently, then followed Aldo's gaze. He was looking at Darwin. Pam's prized cub. "Oh. Right."

26

Spencer climbed back up the tallest tree in Dora's enclosure as Darwin grunted softly in his knotted rope sling, bound tightly to Spencer's chest. Spencer could imagine Dora's ears snapping in the direction of the sound. He knew she was below him now, pacing back and forth, watching his every move to make sure he was being careful with her son.

Spencer's anger at Dora had faded. She hadn't been trying to trick them. She just hadn't realized that Darwin would have to be returned. The risk stealing Darwin posed to the rest of Spencer and Aldo's mission just hadn't mattered to her as much as the chance to see her cub. Spencer had taken the Ear-COM back from Dora and slipped it into his pocket before that conversation. They couldn't leave the top secret device with Dora in case Pam caught sight of it, and Spencer didn't want to hear Aldo reason with the mother bear. He knew Dora would fight for Darwin to stay with her, and he understood why. He couldn't imagine being separated from Mom again after finally being reunited with her, even if just for a short time. But eventually Aldo had convinced Dora that returning Darwin to Pam's house until Bearhaven's team was ready to make its final escape from Hidden Rock Zoo was the only plan that made any sense.

"That's the one," Spencer whispered up to Aldo. The bear was above him, testing the sturdy branch that would carry them all out over the glass wall. Aldo didn't answer; he was just focused on getting out of Dora's home as fast as he could. While Spencer was returning Darwin to his room, Aldo would update B.D. Then Spencer and Aldo would meet in the pear grove as soon as possible, before *finally* going to find Mom, Dad, and Uncle Mark.

"Ready to head back to bed, buddy?" Spencer whispered down to the bundle of black and white fur at his chest. He didn't think the sleepy cub would mind being returned to his fake forest and cave for a little while. Darwin took a long, slow blink.

Once Aldo had reached the tree outside, Spencer climbed out across the wide branch. Just as he was moving deeper into the branches of the far tree, heading for the ground, a fiery sliver of light appeared on the horizon.

"Oh no . . ." he whispered.

"Spencer?"

"The sun's rising," Spencer said, speeding his climb back down to the ground.

"Hurry," Aldo urged, then took off toward the Caves.

Spencer tucked one of Darwin's paws back into place inside the knotted sling and headed for Pam's front path. He pushed open Pam's front door and silent-walked inside. He left the door open behind him. With the sun rising through the massive windows, Spencer didn't need his night-vision goggles to retrace his steps to Darwin's room. This time, he ignored the huge dining room, and the living room filled with bearskin rugs. He headed for the stairs, straining his ears with every step for the sounds of Pam snoring. When he heard the whistling snore, he stepped off the staircase and onto the second floor. He didn't hesitate but rushed down the hall, right into Pam's office, and slipped into Darwin's room. The room was just as he and Darwin had left it barely an hour earlier.

Spencer crouched to the ground. He scooped Darwin out of the rope sling and set him down on all fours. The cub stumbled, then found his footing and trotted over to his cave. He flopped down in the mouth of the cave, gave a great big yawn, and tucked his paws in close to his furry body to sleep.

"So far, so good," Spencer whispered. Quietly, so he wouldn't disturb Darwin, Spencer left the room. Standing in Pam's office, he checked again for the sound of snoring. When he heard it, he headed back downstairs.

Spencer was in the foyer, silent-walking toward Pam's half-open front door when he heard footsteps coming up Pam's front path. He froze. The living room was too wide open, and the thought of hiding anywhere near a bearskin rug made Spencer's own skin crawl. The dining room didn't offer any good hiding spots, either. Spencer turned and sprinted down the long hallway. He saw a doorway and darted through it just as someone stepped through the open front door.

"Hello?" a man's voice called softly. "Hmm. How odd." Spencer held his breath. He immediately regretted leaving the front door open when he'd snuck in. *Just don't alert the guards,* he thought, willing whoever was now in the house with him to not raise an alarm about Pam's open front door. Spencer listened to the door shut. Then footsteps started toward the kitchen.

Now what?! Spencer's heart pounded as he scanned the kitchen. He spotted a pantry on the far side of the room, one of its doors stood open. Spencer ran over to it, ducked inside, and pulled the door shut. Through a small crack between the two pantry doors, Spencer watched a man walk into the kitchen and flip on the lights. He went to one of the cabinets and pulled out a baby bottle.

It's Darwin's caretaker! Spencer realized as he watched the man pull milk from Pam's fridge and heat it in a small pot on the stove. The man checked his watch, filled the baby bottle with warm milk, and left the kitchen.

Spencer sighed in relief. He hadn't been discovered yet, but it was only a matter of time before Pam woke up and the rest of his household staff arrived. Spencer had to get out of here, but first . . . He slipped his mission pack off his back, then grabbed a box of protein bars from a shelf and emptied it into his bag. *Power food for the powerful man* the box read. Spencer rolled his eyes and put the empty box back on its shelf. He took a jar of mixed nuts off another shelf, and a package of dried apricots, hurriedly stuffing them into his mission pack. He zipped the pack and got ready to leave. He didn't know how long it took to bottle-feed a sleepy spirit bear cub, but he definitely didn't want to still be here when Darwin's caretaker got back.

Spencer slowly opened the pantry door, slipped out of the closet, and silent-walked out of Pam's house.

27

"Let's go now, before it's broad daylight," Aldo said, polishing off another pear. His head was bowed beside Spencer's as they crouched in the pear grove and poured over the Hidden Rock Zoo map.

"Of course we should go now!" Spencer exclaimed. *Nothing* was going to delay him going to the aquarium. He pointed to a small open space beside the aviary on the zoo map. "This area must have been left open for the aquarium . . . Come on."

Spencer folded the map and put it in his back pocket. He gathered the empty wrappers from all the protein bars he and Aldo had wolfed down, and stuffed them into his mission pack. Unlike Raymond's fuel bars, these protein bars didn't come with edible wrappers.

"Hop on." Aldo headbutted Spencer.

Spencer grabbed two fistfuls of Aldo's fur and swung himself up onto the bear's back. "Let's go," he said as soon as he was settled. His mind was racing. Until now, it hadn't really felt like Mom and Dad were at Hidden Rock Zoo. There hadn't been a single sign of them, and with the mission going so terribly wrong, Spencer had hardly had a minute to think about how close he really was to his parents. Now Spencer wasn't sure he could go another minute without seeing them.

Aldo broke into a run, and Spencer had to resist urging the bear to go even faster. They flew down the hill into an open field stretching beyond the birdless aviary.

"Do you see an entrance?" Spencer asked. Part of him had expected to find half-constructed buildings here, even though Dora had said the entrance didn't look like much.

"I think so," Aldo said. They were running straight for a set of iron gates, but from what Spencer could tell, there wasn't a building, or anything, beyond the gates. Aldo lurched to a stop. Spencer leaped off the bear's back.

The iron gates didn't lead to a half-constructed building at all. Instead, they led to a sloping cement walkway, and that walkway led straight into the ground. "The aquarium is underground?" he asked.

"It looks like it," Aldo said, then glanced up at the orangey-yellow dawn sky. "We'd better get inside."

Spencer didn't have to be told twice. The iron gates were anchored into low cement walls that rose up on either side of the ramp into the underground aquarium. Spencer climbed up onto the cement wall and hopped down on the other side. Aldo clambered after him, and they set off at a run down the steep path.

At the bottom of the ramp, there were four big doors.

Spencer didn't wait. He couldn't even stop himself long enough for Aldo to smell for humans inside. He reached for the closest door and yanked it open.

Errrr! Errr! Errr! Errr!

An alarm started to blare. Red lights started to flash.

"No!" Spencer shouted.

"Pam must have alarmed it to stop Dora from coming here!" Aldo was frozen a few paces away. "I don't—"

"Come on!" Spencer shouted over the sound of the alarm. He charged into the building.

"Spencer!" Aldo called, ducking in through the open door.

"I have to find my family!" Spencer sprinted into a long tunnel-like hallway that was only illuminated by the red flashing lights of the alarm. "We can't leave now!" Spencer didn't stop to see if Aldo was following. The viewing tunnel was lined in glass windows, like a massive version of the long corridor in the Reptile Lodge. The flashing lights showed dark, empty tanks through the windows.

Did Dora lead us into a trap?!

Where were Mom, Dad, and Uncle Mark? Spencer kept running as fast as he could through the viewing tunnel, swinging his head from side to side, looking into the empty tanks as he passed. For all Spencer knew, the viewing tunnel went for miles. Aldo broke out ahead of Spencer, running on all fours. He disappeared around a bend in the tunnel.

"They have to be here!" Spencer yelled after the bear. The alarm was so loud it was making it hard for him to think straight. He took another turn in the tunnel and spotted Aldo.

"Aldo, what do you see?!" Spencer yelled, wishing his feet could carry him faster. "Where are they?!" Spencer was starting to panic.

"I don't see them yet!" Aldo followed the next curve in

the tunnel and disappeared from sight again. When Spencer finally reached the bend, he found Aldo in a brighter section of the tunnel. It looked like the windows might actually lead to the outside. Spencer's hopes lifted. He forced his legs to move faster, carrying him toward Aldo, who had stopped running and was staring into one of the tanks.

Errrr! Errr! Errr! Errr!

The alarm continued to blare and the lights flashed a threatening red, but when Spencer reached Aldo and the tank the bear was staring into, Spencer forgot the danger they were in. He even forgot the long, winding viewing tunnel they'd just raced through, and Hidden Rock Zoo above them, because in the tank in front of him he saw Mom, Dad, and Uncle Mark.

"Mom!" he yelled at the top of his lungs, pounding his fists against the glass. Mom turned, her blond hair whipping across her face. Her eyes locked on Spencer.

"Spencer!" she cried just as a door banged open somewhere far in the distance in the underground aquarium.

28

Spencer ran down the length of the glass window that stood between himself and the empty tank where Mom, Dad, and Uncle Mark were trapped. He was searching for an opening—a locked door, or a passageway of some kind. Anything that might get him to his family. But there was no way in from the viewing tunnel. All Spencer could do from here was look at Mom, Dad, and Uncle Mark standing inside the cement basin of an empty whale tank. The walls were smooth and high. There were no footholds, no ladders or tools anywhere in sight.

Mom and Dad's mouths were moving inside the tank. They were talking to him, trying to tell him something, but the glass was too thick and the alarm was still blaring, Spencer couldn't understand what they were saying. He stopped running and banged on the glass with both fists as the alarm's red lights flashed over him.

"Someone's coming, Spencer!" Aldo growled urgently. Heavy footsteps echoed through the viewing tunnel, mixing with the harsh *Errrr! Errr!* of the alarm.

"We have to get them out of there!" he shouted.

Mom and Dad both looked exhausted. Their faces were

drawn and thin. Mom's glasses were gone, and her usually sleek blond hair was falling out of a messy ponytail. Spencer had never seen Dad with a beard, but he had one now and his hands were bandaged. He was hurt. Spencer wanted to be with them, in the tank. He didn't care about anything else. He didn't care what happened next, as long as he, Mom, and Dad were together—

"*We* have to get out of here, Spencer!" Aldo growled, cutting into Spencer's thoughts.

In the empty tank, Uncle Mark had started to yell. He looked afraid, and angry. Mom and Dad were looking past Spencer, to the flashing lights, and the viewing tunnel. Spencer pressed an ear to the glass.

"GO NOW!" Uncle Mark was yelling.

"Is somebody here?!" a deep voice shouted. Spencer jumped back from the glass. It was a guard, yelling from around a bend in the viewing tunnel.

"Spencer!" Aldo growled.

Spencer looked at the bear, then at Mom and Dad in the tank. He was panicking. He couldn't think. What was he supposed to do?! If the guards saw them, Pam and his staff would know part of Bearhaven's team was still here.

"Spencer, let's go!" Aldo stepped between Spencer and the bend in the tunnel, as though preparing to protect Spencer when the guards turned the corner.

"I don't see anybody, Guy!" one of the guards yelled. "It's probably Pam's bear like he expected!" The heavy footsteps continued to get closer.

Aldo crouched low, ready to stop the guards. He would fight them if he had to, blocking Spencer from them. But the guards could have weapons. Spencer and Aldo had to make a break for it now, or they would be discovered and then they might never escape. As an operative, Spencer was making the same mistake as B.D. had, putting his team at risk. He couldn't do that to Aldo. If Aldo got captured at Hidden Rock Zoo, he'd be shipped off right away to whatever horrible animal dealer had bought him at the auction last night.

"Let's go!" Spencer hissed. The viewing tunnel hooked to the left behind him. He guessed it made a loop, leading back to the entrance at the bottom of the cement ramp. If they could outrun the guards, staying just far enough ahead to be out of sight—

Aldo turned and paused beside Spencer. Spencer jumped onto Aldo's back. He grabbed two fistfuls of the bear's fur, and the second he did, Aldo launched himself forward, taking off at top speed through the viewing tunnel.

Spencer plastered himself to the running bear. He pressed his face into Aldo's fur and told himself the tears welling in his eyes were from the force of the air whipping into his face as Aldo hurtled forward. But the truth was, Spencer had found Mom and Dad. He'd seen them. He'd been just a few feet away from them. Then he had left them behind. Now he knew exactly how Dora felt.

Before Spencer could think much more about being separated yet again from his family, Aldo was coming to the end of the viewing tunnel. Just as Spencer had thought, it made a wide loop around the underground aquarium and brought them back to the doors they had first come through. One of the doors was open a crack. Aldo barreled straight through it, forcing it open wide with a powerful thrust of his head. The bear rushed through the door, out into the morning sunshine with Spencer holding tightly to his back. He ran up the sloping walkway, hurtled over the low cement wall beside the iron gates, and headed straight for the Reptile Lodge.

29

Spencer and Aldo sat on the floor of the Reptile Lodge, planning their next move. The doors on either end of the building were rigged shut with a network of Spencer's ropes and knots, and they hadn't risked turning on the lights. So far, there hadn't been any sign the guards had spotted Spencer or Aldo as they fled from the aquarium, but they had to be more cautious now than ever.

The Hidden Rock Zoo map was laid out on the ground between them, and a flashlight was propped on the jar of nuts, shining a beam of light down over it. Spencer had a black pen clutched in one hand. They had seen all of Hidden Rock Zoo now. It was time they updated the map.

"Okay, let's start from the beginning," he said. "The front entrance is the same, but there's a guardhouse here." Spencer drew a black square next to the front gates. "The Woodland Walk turned into Pam's gardens." Spencer added the big marble courtyard at the center of the Woodland Walk area of the map, and the waterfall.

"He turned the Shetland Pony Shed into a garage." Aldo pointed to the stables with one claw. Spencer crossed off *Shetland Pony Shed* and wrote *garage*.

"He built his house, and Dora's where the Tropics used to be." Spencer drew the two buildings onto the map. "And the pear grove is here now. And here's the entrance to the underground aquarium," Spencer drew the iron gates and ramp underground in the open space beside the Airy Aviary.

"What's this?" Aldo asked, pointing to a building between the pear grove and the Savanna.

Spencer frowned. "It's labeled *Aqua Theater*," he said. He'd looked at that building on the map at least a hundred times by now, but he'd never thought much about it since it just looked like an empty glass greenhouse when he and Aldo rushed past it. "We've seen it. We were right next to it the first night we were here, when we were searching for Uncle Mark and B.D., but I thought it was just a greenhouse. It looked empty. But why would it be called the Aqua Theater?"

Aldo and Spencer both fell silent. Could the Aqua Theater have something to do with the aquarium? Spencer thought back to the one time he'd been to an aquarium. He'd gone with his two best friends from home, Cheng and Ramona, and Cheng's dad. They had walked all throughout the aquarium, looking through the thick glass windows into tanks filled with fish and sea turtles and eels and all sorts of water creatures. Then Spencer remembered the dolphin show. They'd gone to a little arena above the dolphin tank, and watched the dolphins do tricks.

"Wait a second . . ." Spencer whispered. "Aldo, when we were in the aquarium, wasn't the tank Mom, Dad, and Uncle Mark were in different than the others?"

Aldo was quiet. "Yes," he said after a second. "It had

daylight! The others were dark. But their tank opened up to the outdoors somehow."

Spencer looked down at the map. He traced his finger from the parking lot where Dora had attacked B.D. to the Aqua Theater. "That explains why Margo and Ivan took Uncle Mark and B.D. over there when they captured them. And why you suddenly lost their scent!"

"What?" Aldo asked, trying to follow Spencer's logic.

"Okay, so at aquariums, they do these shows where dolphins and whales perform tricks. And people sit in the stands above the tank and watch. The Aqua Theater must have been built for shows! And the tank inside is where they're keeping Mom, Dad, and Uncle Mark!" Spencer started to get excited.

"And this is good news?" Aldo asked.

"Yes! It means we know how to get to them! The tank has to be open at the top. It opens into the Aqua Theater!" Spencer drew an X over the Aqua Theater and wrote *Mom, Dad, Uncle Mark*. "And we know B.D. is here." He put an X over the Caves and wrote *B.D.* "And Dora and Darwin are here, and here," Spencer finished, marking Dora and Pam's homes for the last two bears.

Spencer put the black pen down. He had drawn four Xs on the map, and those four Xs represented the six rescues he and Aldo needed to make.

"I think we need more operatives," Aldo said solemnly, staring down at the map.

"What did you say?" Spencer asked. A plan was starting to take shape in his mind.

"I said I think we need more operatives," Aldo repeated.

"Three humans and three bears need to be rescued, and there are only two of us." The bear lowered his head closer to the map, obviously trying to come up with a plan himself.

"I think you're onto something," Spencer said slowly. "The thing is, we *do* have a lot of operatives here. Mom, Dad, Uncle Mark, and B.D. are all highly trained operatives. Plus you and me. We probably shouldn't count B.D. because of his injuries, but just because three of our operatives are at the bottom of a whale tank in the Aqua Theater doesn't mean they can't help us on this mission!"

"What do you mean?" Aldo asked.

"I mean, I don't think we have to rescue Mom, Dad, and Uncle Mark from the whale tank."

Aldo looked at Spencer like he'd suggested they pack up and leave everyone behind.

"I *mean* we just have to give them the tools they need to rescue themselves!" Spencer explained.

"You're right!" Aldo exclaimed.

"You said teamwork was going to get us out of Hidden Rock Zoo," Spencer continued. "We just need to figure out how to activate the other half of the team."

30

Spencer and Aldo sifted through the contents of Spencer's mission pack. They had made their plan. Now it was time to make sure they had everything they needed to put that plan in motion.

"Okay, so let's review," Spencer said. "Step one, in the middle of the night tonight, you are going to run right past the guardhouse acting like a crazy escaped bear. You don't need any tools, and you'll leave your Ear-COM with me."

"Right," Aldo agreed. Spencer didn't like the idea of being disconnected from Aldo, but he knew if anything went wrong, and Aldo got captured, they couldn't risk the Ear-COM falling into Pam's hands. *Aldo is* not *going to get captured,* Spencer promised himself.

"Step two, when the guards follow you, I'll sneak into the guardhouse to shut down the signal blockers around the zoo so we can communicate with Evarita again. I'll open the front gates and disable as many of the security systems as I can. I'll need tools." Spencer pushed a hammer, a screwdriver, and a pair of scissors into a little pile. "I'll also tell Mom, Dad, and Uncle Mark to escape from the tank. For their escape, they'll need a lot of rope, something they can use as a grappling hook, and an Ear-COM."

Spencer grabbed B.D.'s Ear-COM from the pile of supplies and slipped it into his pocket for safekeeping. Both of his lengths of rope were tying the Reptile Lodge doors shut, and he would need them later for Darwin. "We need to find another supply of rope and a hook somewhere."

"Right." Aldo nodded.

"Step three, after Mom, Dad, and Uncle Mark are free, they're going to the pool shed to hide out, since it's the closest building to the front gates, and nobody will be there in the middle of the night. You'll meet them there, after you lose the guards. Step four, I'll go get Darwin out of Pam's house and bring him to Dora, who can get them both to the pool shed. For that, I just need rope and an Ear-COM. I have two coils of rope, and I'll have your Ear-COM by then."

"Okay," Aldo said. "The last rescue is B.D."

"Yes," Spencer agreed. "Step five, after I send Dora and Darwin to you in the pool shed, I'll go get B.D. I'll need the lock-picking kit." Spencer dug the lock-picking kit out of the pile of supplies and added it to the tools he'd already set aside. "B.D. and I will get to the pool house. Step six, we charge the front gates as a team. Evarita will be waiting outside with a getaway vehicle."

"We hope," Aldo said.

"We hope," Spencer repeated solemnly. He didn't want to think about what they would have to do if Evarita wasn't ready to evacuate them all . . . And he also didn't know what kind of vehicle she would be able to find on such short notice that could fit three bears, a cub, and five people. *Everything will go according to plan,* he told himself, pushing his doubts away. *It has to.*

"So our first move is to find a supply of rope and a hook, probably in the pool shed," Aldo said, breaking the silence. "Then we'll drop it off for Jane, Shane, and Mark, and camp out near the guardhouse until midnight."

"We'll leave after dark," Spencer replied, pulling his empty mission pack onto his lap.

"All right." Aldo leaned back, settling himself against the wall, and closed his eyes. "I'm going to get some rest while I can."

"Me too." Spencer set the last of his food supply—two protein bars and the jar of mixed nuts—and his phone to the side, and started to put the rest of his things back into his mission pack with the tools he knew he would need tonight right on top. When his bag was totally packed, Spencer set the alarm on his phone for ten o'clock p.m. He leaned back against the wall to get a few hours of sleep. Aldo was already snoring beside him.

Spencer felt like he'd only just fallen asleep when the alarm on his phone startled him awake.

Aldo's eyes shot open.

Pop! Aldo gave a jaw pop and lurched forward, getting to all fours. He quickly rose onto his hind legs and glared around the Reptile Lodge, sniffing hard. His ears twitched.

"Aldo!" Spencer cried. "It's okay! It was my phone!"

"What?" Aldo dropped back to all fours.

"That sound," Spencer explained. "It was just the alarm from my phone. We aren't being attacked or anything."

"Oh, thank goodness!" Aldo relaxed. "Next time, give a bear a little warning, okay? I thought we were done for."

"I'm sorry." Spencer stifled a laugh. "You fell asleep before I could tell you I set the alarm. I didn't want us to oversleep."

"Time to go?" Aldo asked.

"Almost." Spencer unwrapped one of the protein bars and handed it to Aldo, then took the top off the jar of mixed nuts and dumped the nuts out into a little pile on top of the empty wrapper on the ground. The bear swallowed the bar in one bite, and wolfed down the pile of nuts before Spencer was even halfway through his own protein bar. He finished the rest as quickly as he could, then set to work untying the doors to the Reptile Lodge, and recoiling his rope.

Spencer could feel his excitement starting to build. Tonight, they were going to get out of Hidden Rock Zoo once and for all, and they were taking everyone they came here to rescue with them.

31

Spencer hung on tight to Aldo's back as the bear made his way to the pool shed. They were sticking to the perimeter of the dark zoo, and though Spencer was trying to stay alert and watch for guards, security cameras, or anything else that might give them away, he could hardly see a thing, especially when they raced through the alleyway between Hidden Rock Zoo's outer wall and the Caves.

I am definitely going to need the night-vision goggles tonight, he thought, glad for the millionth time that he'd brought the cool gear along on this mission.

Aldo broke out of the alley and headed for the Seaport Pools. On the hilltop to their right, Spencer could see lights on in Pam's house. He hoped now, of all times, Pam wasn't standing on his second-floor viewing deck, surveying his miniature world . . .

When they reached the shed beside the Seaport Pools area of the zoo, Spencer slid off Aldo's back. Each pool was lit from below, and each one looked like a moon, glowing silver into the dark night. The nearest pool cast enough light for Spencer to find the door to the pool shed. Remembering his impatience to enter the aquarium, and the alarm he'd set off in the process, Spencer paused, waiting for Aldo to smell the door.

The bear finished his scent investigation. "Nobody's here," he said. Spencer pushed open the door, bracing himself for an alarm to blare on, but the door swung open in silence. He let out a sigh of relief and stepped into the little building. He pulled the flashlight from his back pocket and flicked it on.

"This would have made a much better hideout," Aldo whispered when the first thing the flashlight's beam landed on was a pile of lounge chair cushions. "It would have been way more comfortable."

"Okay, let's look for rope and a hook." Spencer maneuvered around the pile of cushions and a pile of folded-up umbrellas. It looked like all kinds of supplies were stored in this building. He scanned a huge set of shelves filled with cleaning supplies, then moved on to a tall stack of cardboard boxes. He pulled one of the boxes down and flipped the top open.

Black gift boxes were neatly stacked inside, each one imprinted with the silver crown logo. Spencer couldn't look at it now without thinking about Darwin, even though Pam's plan for the cub still puzzled Spencer.

He opened one of the gift boxes. Inside, surrounded by velvet cushioning, was a black stone bear figurine. Spencer felt goose bumps rise on his arms. The figurine looked so much like his own jade bear. The bear was standing up on its hind legs, just like Spencer's jade figurine. A jeweled collar had been carved onto its neck, and on its head, in shining silver, was a crown.

Spencer lifted the figurine out of its box. It was at least three times bigger than his jade bear. Beneath the bear, the velvet was embroidered. *King of Bears* it read. Spencer thought of Darwin again, the living version of this stone figurine and suddenly he understood exactly what Pam's plans for Darwin were. *Pam is just going to use Darwin to show off his power over bears*, he thought with disgust. "What a creepy party favor," Spencer said aloud.

"What?" Aldo's voice rang in Spencer's ear. The bear was on the other side of the shed.

"Oh, nothing." Spencer dropped the bear figurine back into its velvet-padded box, and closed it up. He didn't need to think about Pam's plans for Darwin, or the evil work he did at Moon Farm, because tonight's rescue was going to be the first step in stopping Pam's plans altogether. It had to be.

"I think I found something," Aldo called. Spencer pointed his flashlight in the direction of Aldo's grunts. The bear had a long coil of pool lane dividers looped around his neck. He was holding one end up in his claws. "Looks like rope to me."

"Perfect!" Spencer exclaimed. He made his way over to Aldo, who had found a pile of five pool rope lane dividers. "Let's bring two, just in case." Spencer took the lane divider from around Aldo's neck. He popped off the plastic buoys one by one, leaving only the thin, strong nylon rope of the lane divider. Then he started to coil the rope into the tightest ball he could. "Now we need a hook."

Aldo padded deeper into the shed. A minute later, he returned. Spencer shone his flashlight on the bear, who was sitting back on his haunches, a huge garden tool in his claws.

"I think Raymond has one of these," Aldo said, examining the oversized garden fork. Spencer laughed with relief. It was definitely bear-sized, but after seeing how big Pam's gardens were, Spencer wasn't surprised there was such a tool at Hidden Rock Zoo. The garden fork had a long wooden handle and a metal head with four curved prongs. It was exactly what they needed. They could use this garden tool as a grappling hook to send down to Mom and Dad and Uncle Mark.

"All right, we have everything," Spencer said. "Now we just need to get it all to them." Spencer reached for the garden fork. It was way too sharp to drop into the empty tank the way it was. He took the second lane divider and used it to wrap the tines of the heavy fork tool. When he was halfway done, Spencer remembered the Ear-COM. They had to find a way to drop it safely, too. "I have an idea!" He rushed back over to the boxes of bear figurines and grabbed one. *These creepy gifts are good for something after all!* he thought, opening the box. The stone figure glared at him. Spencer grabbed it and shoved it deep into his pocket, where the jade bear was supposed to be. He hurried back to where Aldo was waiting with the other supplies. "Look," he said, shining the flashlight into the velvet interior of the box.

"For the Ear-COM?" Aldo guessed. "Good thinking."

Spencer grabbed B.D.'s Ear-COM from his pocket and placed it inside the small gift box. He put the box on top of the garden fork with the partially wrapped tines. "Can you hold this here?" he asked Aldo. Aldo extended a claw, pinning down the gift box to the garden fork. Spencer continued to wind the lane divider around the garden fork, wrapping the Ear-COM in its protective box into the bundle. Aldo removed his claw when the box was secure. "Okay. All set," Spencer said, knotting the last bit of rope to the garden fork's handle. He stood up. The garden fork looked like half of a giant Q-tip. Spencer picked it up and swung it onto his shoulder, propping it there. "I can carry this. Can you get the other lane divider?"

"Sure," Aldo answered, eyeing the garden fork on Spencer's shoulder. "We're going to have to be extra careful now."

"I know," Spencer answered, looking up at the white rope. "This thing looks like a white flag, but we are definitely *not* planning to surrender."

32

Getting from the pool shed to the Aqua Theater took forever. Because of the tools they were transporting, and the way the lane-divider-wrapped garden fork ended in a bright white bulb, Aldo and Spencer again had to stick to the darkest part of Hidden Rock Zoo—its perimeter—and this time, Spencer couldn't ride on Aldo's back. He had to walk on his own two feet.

When the Aqua Theater finally came into view, Spencer was so happy he wanted to cheer. He was about to see Mom and Dad again, and he was finally going to show them he had become a full-blown Bearhaven operative since their disappearance. He could hardly wait.

"Spencer, hold on," Aldo whispered, hanging back in the shadows of Alligator Alley. He'd dropped the coil of rope he'd been carrying to the ground. "I don't think we should both go into the Aqua Theater. One of us should stand guard."

"Okay, I'll go," Spencer said right away.

"Well . . ." Aldo hesitated.

"What?"

"Are you sure you'll be able to stay calm? And think like an operative?" Aldo asked. Then he rushed on. "It's just that after what happened with B.D., and then in the aquarium . . ."

"I can do this, Aldo," he said. "I promise I won't let my emotions get in the way again." Spencer picked up the coil of rope. Through the night-vision goggles, it looked like a bright green soccer ball. "You stand guard. I'm going in."

"All right," Aldo agreed. "I'll wait in the pear grove. It's closer to the Aqua Theater, and I'll be able to see more from there. Let me go first. Once I'm in position, I'll give you the signal to go."

"Okay," Spencer said, though he hated the idea of waiting even another five minutes before delivering the rescue tools to Mom, Dad, and Uncle Mark. Aldo loped out of the swampy, overgrown protection of Alligator Alley.

The bear's voice was in Spencer's ear a few minutes later. "I'm in position. Go ahead."

"Got it," Spencer whispered. He adjusted the garden fork on his shoulder and tucked the ball of coiled rope under one arm. If he got intercepted by guards halfway between Alligator Alley and the Aqua Theater, he would be in deep trouble. With all this gear he was carrying, he wasn't exactly going to be able to run for it. Spencer crept out of Alligator Alley and onto the path winding through the zoo. There wasn't much to protect him from view, just a few trees, so Spencer went as quickly as he could. When he reached the Aqua Theater, he found a set of glass double doors.

"Aldo," he hissed, suddenly starting to panic. "What if the doors are alarmed like the other entrance?!" Spencer couldn't believe they hadn't thought of it before!

"Do you see any other way in?" Aldo asked. Spencer scanned the glass building.

"The windows at the top are open . . ." Spencer whispered, though he'd rather try his luck digging his way in with the garden fork—anything other than climb.

"Can you get to one of them?"

"I think so," Spencer answered reluctantly. The walls of the Aqua Theater were made of panels of glass, and each panel was set into an iron frame. Spencer could scale the wall, using the iron frames as a ladder. He just *really* didn't want to.

"You can do it, Spencer," Aldo urged as though reading Spencer's mind.

Spencer took a deep breath and sprang into action. He knew the less he thought about the climb, the better it would go. He unraveled the lane divider and tied one end to the garden fork, and the other to one of the straps on his mission pack.

Spencer reached for the lowest bar of one of the iron frames and hooked one foot over it, then reached for the next highest bar, pushing himself up the wall. The long coil of rope stayed slack between him and the garden fork on the ground below, just as he'd hoped. Frame by frame, Spencer climbed the glass wall. He tried to think about only the next step in the plan—giving Mom, Dad, and Uncle Mark the tools they needed to escape—and before he knew it, he had reached the window. Spencer hooked one leg inside the building, finding a stable seat on the window frame.

"Good work, little man," Aldo said through the Ear-COMs.

"Thanks." Spencer felt a little more confident knowing

Aldo was watching him so closely. He reached for the long rope that attached his mission pack to the garden fork.

Slowly, and careful to keep his arms extended so the garden fork wouldn't smash into the glass wall, Spencer began to pull up the fork. It felt like all the muscles in his body were working. He gritted his teeth. Eventually, Spencer was able to grab hold of the garden fork's handle, pull it inside, and quickly lower it to the floor.

"All right, now for the hard part," he whispered, trying not to look down.

"What's the hard part?" Aldo asked.

"Climbing down the other side." Spencer looked down. His stomach lurched.

"Good luck."

Spencer took a deep breath. With both hands gripping the window frame he was perched on, he got a foothold on an iron rung inside the building. He swung his other leg inside and started to climb down until he hopped off the last bar and landed with a soft thud.

"I'm in," he whispered. He rushed over to the side of the tank and dropped to his knees. "Mom! Dad! Uncle Mark!" he whispered. They were all standing in a row at the bottom of the tank below, looking up at him, as though preparing to react to whatever happened next. *They must have heard me coming!* he thought.

"Spencer!" his parents whispered back up to him at the same time.

"Are you okay?" Spencer asked, his voice hushed but bubbling over with the excitement of finally talking face-to-face with Mom and Dad even though they were forty feet below.

"Yes, we are!" Mom answered.

"We're okay, Spencer," Dad added. "But is it safe for you to be here?"

"Where's Aldo, Spence?" Uncle Mark called up.

Spencer wanted to jump down into the tank and hug his family. He wanted to change the plan and get them out of the tank now, but he remembered what he'd promised Aldo. He wouldn't let his emotions get in the way tonight.

"Aldo's standing guard. We're escaping tonight," Spencer whispered, leaning down over the side of the tank and getting right to the point. "All of us. Hold on!" Spencer scooted backward and ran to retrieve the garden fork and rope. As he rushed back to the side of the tank, he was relieved to see a short metal ladder was anchored into the cement surrounding the tank. The plan he and Aldo had come up with for Mom, Dad, and Uncle Mark's escape was going to work. The ladder led a few feet down, just like a ladder in a human pool—though, the bottom of the tank was *way* farther down than the bottom of a human pool—and the marine animal trainers would have used the ladder to get into the tank with the whales for shows. He remembered that from his trip to the aquarium with Cheng and Ramona. Spencer untied the rope from his mission pack.

"Watch out!" he called, lowering the garden fork into the tank. When it hit the floor, Spencer dropped the rest of the length of rope in on top. "That's everything you'll need, including an Ear-COM," he explained. "Keep it all hidden however you can until I give you the signal to go, in case someone comes to check on you."

"Got it, Spence," Uncle Mark replied. He strode over to the pile of supplies and started to unwind the rope around the garden fork. Spencer guessed he was searching for the Ear-COM. Before Spencer could call down about where to find it, Dad's voice was rising up out of the tank.

"You're sure you're safe, Spencer?" Dad called.

"I'm sure, Dad. Don't worry, Aldo and I have a plan. We're getting out of here tonight!"

"Spencer, if anything goes wrong, I want you to get yourself out of Hidden Rock Zoo. Do you understand?" Mom asked, her voice firm. "We'll be fine."

"Mom, nothing's going to go wrong. We have something Pam doesn't have."

"What's that?" Dad asked.

"Wanmahai."

33

Spencer was halfway down the glass wall, on the outside of the Aqua Theater when he suddenly panicked. He hadn't lost his grip. Nothing about his climb down from the open window at the top of the wall had changed. But he'd *thought* about falling, and now he couldn't shake the images out of his head.

Not now! He tried to push it away, but before he knew it, the memory that always made him panic when he was climbing hit him. He squeezed his eyes shut and held tight to the wall as the images crashed into his head.

He was being carried roughly up into a tall tree by a furious bear, his head was scraped and bleeding. He was struggling to get away, then he fell, careening toward the ground, rushing faster and faster through leaves and branches and—

"Team." Mom's voice was suddenly in Spencer's ear. He blinked his eyes open. He was panting, still holding firmly to an iron ledge, halfway between the window at the top of the Aqua Theater and the ground. He wasn't falling through trees. He wasn't reliving the moment when he had fallen from Yude's clutches on his first trip to Bearhaven as a child. That first visit to Bearhaven had changed everything, making

155

Mom and Dad think they had to keep Spencer safe from Bearhaven by keeping it a secret from him. Spencer wasn't back there now. He was in control.

"Mom." He breathed a sigh of relief, then continued his climb to the ground.

"Spencer, I'm about to turn the Ear-COM over to your uncle so he can finish out this mission in communication with you, but I need you to know—"

"Yeah?" Spencer hopped to the ground and set off at a jog toward the pear grove.

"You can trust Dora."

Spencer hesitated. The memory of Dora attacking B.D. flashed into his mind, and then the way she'd made Spencer risk going into Pam's house twice to get and then return Darwin, and the way she'd sent them into the aquarium without warning them it was alarmed . . . Spencer and Aldo planned to rescue Dora tonight . . . but could they trust her?

"You're sure?" Aldo's voice suddenly chimed in. Spencer had forgotten the bear's Ear-COM was connected as well.

"Yes, Aldo," Mom answered. "I'm sure."

"Okay," Spencer whispered, jogging up the hill and into the pear grove.

"Be smart tonight," Mom said. "Both of you." Then, after a pause, she added, *"Abragan."*

"Abragan." Spencer puffed up with pride. Mom had spoken to him in Ragayo, like he was a real operative.

"For the bears," Aldo said, his growls translating through the Ear-COMs.

"Here's Mark."

Spencer crept around the outskirts of the pear grove, searching the tree branches for Aldo. "I'm at the edge of the pear grove, Aldo," he whispered. "Where are you?"

A pear dropped to the ground a few inches from Spencer. He jumped aside and looked up. Aldo was there. A second later, the bear's head extended down from some of the lowest branches. He grabbed the back of Spencer's T-shirt between his teeth and hoisted Spencer up into the tree.

"Oof! I could have climbed up here myself," Spencer whispered as he settled himself on a branch.

"I've never heard you say that before, Spence." Uncle Mark's voice suddenly came over the Ear-COM.

"Uncle Mark!" Spencer whispered, happy to have his uncle back in communication.

"So what's the plan, gentlemen?"

"We're heading to the guardhouse soon." Aldo immediately launched into the plan. "I'm going to act as a distraction. Spencer's going to get inside and try to reestablish communication with Evarita. He'll let you know when to start your escape. You, Shane, and Jane just need to focus on getting yourselves out of the tank and over to the pool shed. Do you know where it is?"

"Jane, do you know where the pool shed is?" Uncle Mark said. Then, a moment later, "Yes, we know where it is."

"Okay," Aldo continued. "We're eventually all going to meet there. You three, B.D.—"

"What's B.D.'s condition?" Uncle Mark asked.

"He's hurt," Spencer jumped in. "But I'm going to help him get to the pool shed."

"We'll also have Dora and her cub," Aldo added.

"Jane told me about the cub," said Uncle Mark. "We can't leave here without him."

"We won't," Spencer confirmed.

"Once we've all met in the pool shed, we'll make our final escape. Evarita will be ready with a getaway vehicle," Aldo finished.

"All right. We'll wait for your instructions to go, Spence."

"Okay." Spencer looked at Aldo. "We should get moving."

"See you in the pool shed, Mark," Aldo said.

"We'll be there."

34

Spencer and Aldo crouched in the dark beside Hidden Rock Zoo's outer wall. They had the guardhouse in sight. They were ready.

Almost.

All that was left to do before starting the escape mission was to remove Aldo's Ear-COM. But as soon as they did, Spencer and Aldo wouldn't be able to communicate. They had gotten this far together, as a team. The idea of separating now seemed like a flaw in the plan.

"All right," Aldo said. "I guess it's now or never. If we wait too long, the sun's going to rise."

"Yup," Spencer said. "This was the plan."

"This *is* the plan. It's a good plan. It's going to work." Aldo sounded like he was trying to convince himself as much as he was trying to reassure Spencer. "We make a good team, little man," Aldo said, headbutting Spencer in the shoulder. "Now let's finish this mission so we can all go home." The bear bowed his head.

"You're right. Let's finish this mission." Spencer took Aldo's Ear-COM from the bear's ear and slipped it into his pocket. Aldo nodded, then started toward the guardhouse.

Spencer followed. When they got close, Spencer dropped to his hands and knees and crept into position beneath one of the open windows on the side of the small building.

Aldo paused. He started to huff and snort loudly. The sounds of chairs moving came out of the guardhouse. The second they did, Aldo lurched forward and lumbered around the side of the building. He gave another aggressive grunt and snort.

"Ahhh!!!" A scream sounded from the guardhouse. Spencer smiled, then heard the thundering footsteps of a bear breaking into a run.

"Stop screaming!" a guard shouted. "One of the bears is out! We gotta get him before Pam finds out! Come on!" Spencer listened to more commotion, more shouts, then footsteps running into the distance. He leaped up and darted around the side of the guardhouse. He slipped in the front door and closed it behind himself, pushing the night-vision goggles up to the top of his head.

Spencer scanned the bright one-room building. One wall had a huge bank of surveillance screens. It looked like there were fifty camera feeds. He ran over, scanning each one quickly. At first, Spencer was confused. He didn't see *any* of the buildings or pathways he knew made up Hidden Rock Zoo. The footage on almost every screen looked the same: dry empty land dotted with shrubs and a few trees. Then he understood. Pam's surveillance was like Bearhaven's. His cameras were trained on the exterior of Hidden Rock Zoo. It looked like they lined the top of the tall stone wall surrounding the property, and they were all pointed out, searching for possible intruders. Dora had been right.

Pam's security was focused on not letting anyone into his secret zoo. From what Spencer could tell, there wasn't *any* surveillance of the inside of the zoo.

The screens weren't a threat to the mission right now, so Spencer couldn't waste time on them. He ran to the opposite side of the room where there was a high-tech panel that looked like a map of the property. The outer wall was lined with little red lights, as was the aquarium and Dora's home. The tiny bulbs outlining each of the other buildings on the property were dark. "This must be the alarm system," Spencer whispered. There were switches running all along one side of the control panel. They were labeled in numbers Spencer didn't recognize, but three of them were switched on. He snapped them off. The red lights went dark.

"Team!" he whispered urgently, connecting to the Ear-COM in Uncle Mark's ear.

"Now, Spence?" Uncle Mark said immediately.

"Now!"

"All right, we're moving," Uncle Mark said. "Disconnect."

Spencer spun around. He needed to find the signal blockers. There was another control panel to his right. He moved over to it and quickly found the button to open the front gates, but he didn't need that yet. All the buttons or switches were labeled, but none of them read *signal blocker*.

Spencer frantically searched the room. A big metal box hummed in one corner. Spencer raced over to it. A small label on the top corner read *800 MHz Large-Range Blocker*.

"Yes!" Spencer cheered to himself. But a thick plastic case was secured over the on and off switches, sealing them into a protective box of their own. A row of tiny screws held the switch cover to the metal signal blocker. It would take Spencer forever to unscrew them all!

Spencer dropped his mission pack to the ground. He quickly pulled out his screwdriver and hammer, then pushed his night-vision goggles down over his eyes.

"Here goes nothing," he whispered. Spencer pressed the point of the screwdriver to the center of the plastic box covering the switches. He wound up and hit the handle of the screwdriver with the hammer as hard as he could.

Crack! A crack appeared in the plastic.

Spencer hit the screwdriver again.

Crack! The crack deepened.

Again Spencer put all his muscle behind slamming the hammer down on the butt of the screwdriver.

Crack!

"Yes!" The screwdriver broke through the plastic. Spencer twisted it in the crack he'd made until the tip of the screwdriver was positioned over the OFF button and jammed it down. The metal box stopped humming.

"Evarita," Spencer said. *Please work.*

After a moment went by without an answer from Evarita, Spencer's hands started to sweat. What would they do if they couldn't reach her? How would they get away once they made it through the front gates?! "Evarita!" he called, getting desperate.

"Spencer?! Oh, thank goodness! Spencer, where are you? What's going on?" It was Evarita. Spencer had done it! But before Spencer could respond, another voice was in the room.

"Guards!" It was Pam, blaring out of speaker beside the door. "Meet me at the Aqua Theater right away."

Spencer's heart started to pound. Pam was on his way to the Aqua Theater! He must have found out about the escape!

"Spencer?" Evarita was in his ear. Spencer opened his mouth to answer her, but Pam's voice filled the room again. There was a sharp edge in his usually syrupy tone.

"Guards! Did you hear me?"

35

"Evarita, hold on," Spencer whispered. He was standing in the guardhouse, his hands sweating and his heart hammering in his chest. He stared at the intercom system beside the door. Pam was waiting for an answer to his demand that the guards meet him at the Aqua Theater. But the guards weren't here, only Spencer was.

Spencer reached a shaking finger toward the button marked TALK. He pressed it.

"Got it, boss," he said in his deepest possible voice, desperately hoping he would sound like one of Pam's guards. He took his hand off the button, and braced himself for Pam's answer.

"Good," Pam said. "And step on it. We have a problem."

Spencer tried to calm down, but he couldn't. His *Got it, boss* had fooled Pam, but now Pam was on the way to catch Mom, Dad, and Uncle Mark in the middle of their escape!

"Evarita!" he gasped remembering he needed to tell her what to do. "I don't have long."

"Okay, I'm listening," Evarita replied. "What's going on?"

"We're all okay. B.D. is injured, but we're all okay," the words poured out of Spencer. "We're escaping tonight but the Creative Pastry truck is gone. Can you get a new getaway vehicle? There are going to be four humans, three bears, and one cub. I'm about to open the front gates. Can you be ready to get us out of here?"

"Yes," Evarita answered. "How long do I have?"

Spencer raced over to the signal blocker. He shoved his hammer back into his mission pack, zipped the bag, and slung it onto his back.

"An hour, maybe."

"I'm on it," Evarita answered.

Spencer ran to the control panel with the button for the front gates. He slammed his palm down on the button and heard the gates creaking open outside.

"Great. I have to go," Spencer said as he pushed open the door to the guardhouse and sprinted outside. "Disconnect."

Spencer turned left and ran as hard as he could down the front drive, under the tree tunnel. He had to head Pam off. Luckily, he could guess what route Pam would take from his house to the Aqua Theater. Spencer turned left at the massive bear fountain. He didn't have time to think about his legs burning, or his chest heaving as he sprinted past the pools, then past the Caves. He forced himself to keep moving.

He hurtled up Pam's front steps, then cut off toward the pear grove as soon as he'd reached the hilltop. He pushed his night-vision goggles up onto his forehead as he ran. The entire pear grove was illuminated. Lights twinkled from each tree. At the very end of the grove, he could see Pam, with Dora padding on all fours beside him. They were heading for the Aqua Theater. They were about to break out of the trees and walk into plain sight.

"PAM!" Spencer screamed. He kept running straight at Pam and Dora. They both spun around to face Spencer.

WHY DID I DO THAT?! Spencer started to panic. He didn't have a plan yet, but he didn't want Pam to get a view of the Aqua Theater. He had to keep him in the pear grove. But now Pam was staring at Spencer, and he didn't look happy. Dora huffed beside Pam.

"You can trust Dora," Mom had said. Spencer really hoped she was right. Dora huffed again as Spencer approached. She rose onto her hind legs, staring at Spencer. Spencer wished he could reach for his jade bear now, but he knew all that was in his pocket was the crowned bear figurine. And that *definitely* wouldn't make him feel better about what he was about to do.

"Now, now, Dora," Pam said, his singsongy voice returned. "You can't eat a child as a midnight snack." Dora remained on her hind legs, looming beside Pam, who hadn't taken his eyes off Spencer.

"Black bears don't eat humans," Spencer said spitefully, slowing to a stop a few yards from Pam and Dora.

"Maybe not in *Bearhaven* they don't." The way Pam said *Bearhaven* made Spencer's skin crawl.

"What do you know about Bearhaven?" he shot back.

"A lot more than you all want me to know." Pam used one of his clawlike nails to put a lock of black hair back into place. Spencer saw him cast an anxious glance toward the Aqua Theater. *He's looking for his guards,* Spencer thought. Pam's eyes snapped back to Spencer. "What I haven't figured out yet is why you and your family insist on delivering yourselves to me on silver platters. Don't you realize your bear friends need you now more than ever?"

Spencer could feel himself boiling with anger. "Leave Bearhaven alone!" he shouted furiously.

Dora huffed again. She dropped to all fours and lunged toward Spencer, stepping between him and Pam.

Pam laughed from behind Dora. "Maybe a midnight snack wouldn't be so bad after all." Dora rose back onto her hind legs, chuffing threateningly.

It took all of Spencer's willpower not to scream and run from Dora, but something about the way she was looking at him made him think the scene she was making wasn't what it seemed. And Mom had promised that Dora was trustworthy.

She huffed aggressively again. Spencer couldn't see Pam behind her. Dora was completely blocking Pam's view, too.

"*Shala,*" she growled. At the bear's word for "safe," Spencer knew Dora was working with him, not against him. The bear let out a loud whine and suddenly went rigid. She staggered on her hind legs, then collapsed to the ground.

"Dora!" Pam cried. He glared at Spencer. "What did you do to her?" he snarled.

Spencer's mouth went dry. What was Dora's plan?! What did she want him to do next?! "I . . . I . . ." he stammered, trying to figure out how to make Dora's collapse help him. His mind raced. Pam was frozen in place, glaring at him.

"Guards!" Pam yelled.

Then Spencer had it. He grabbed one of the coils of rope that was clipped to the side of his mission pack. "If you're going to hurt my bears, I'm not going to be any nicer to yours," he said through gritted teeth. He started to tie a knot in his length of rope as he moved closer to Dora.

"My guards will be here any second," Pam threatened. "If you so much as lay a finger on my bear—"

Spencer lunged toward Dora with his rope tied in a running knot, the loop at the top left open. Pam lunged forward, too, falling for Spencer's fake move. He reached out a hand to stop Spencer from tying Dora up. Spencer slipped the loop over Pam's outstretched hand and yanked it tight, knotting it around Pam's wrist.

"What are you doing?!" Pam screamed. "Guards!" he yelled again.

"Your guards are busy!" Spencer yelled. He charged forward, launching himself over Dora's slumped body, and grabbed Pam around the knees, toppling him to the ground.

"Dora!" Pam yelled, but Dora didn't move. "Guards!" Pam tried to scramble to his feet. Spencer rushed to the closest tree. It was only a few feet from where Pam had fallen. He tossed the rope that was tied tightly around one of Pam's wrists, over a low tree branch, then pulled it back down. He did a lap around the trunk with the rope. Pam was struggling to his feet when Spencer got back to him. But there was nowhere Pam could go, with one of his arms already bound to the tree. Spencer ran straight into Pam, knocking the man back against the tree trunk. Pam slashed out with the nails of his free hand, but Spencer dodged the blow from Pam's claws. He had Pam pinned to the tree now with his rope. He did another lap around the trunk, then grabbed Pam's free arm and tied that wrist, too.

"Ahh!" Spencer cried as Pam's long creepy nails pierced the skin on the back of his hand. He continued to tie knots, ignoring the blood, until he'd bound Pam's body and both of his hands to the tree.

"I don't know what you think you're doing," Pam hissed. "But this will be the end of you. When I take Bearhaven, *nobody* will be spared."

Spencer tried to ignore Pam. He took off his mission pack and dug the long blond haired wig out from the bottom of his bag.

"You better be careful what you say to me," Spencer threatened, trying to sound as dangerous as possible. "Or you may never see Dora again." With that, he yanked the blond wig down hard on top of Pam's head, making sure it was on backward. The mass of blond hair blocked Pam's sight.

"Guards!" Pam yelled at the top of his lungs.

Spencer grabbed his mission pack and returned to Dora's side. He knelt down beside her and laid a hand on her shoulder. Dora opened her eyes. Spencer jerked his head in the direction of her home, then took off at a run. A second later, Dora caught up with him. The sound of Pam yelling for his guards over and over again drowned out their footsteps.

36

As soon as Spencer and Dora reached Dora's home, Spencer pulled Aldo's Ear-COM out of his pocket and held it out in the palm of his hand. Dora stepped closer to Spencer, offering him her ear, and he placed the translating device inside.

"Aldo," he said right away, connecting his Ear-COM with the one that had been programmed for Aldo, but was now in Dora's ear. "Thank you, Dora," he went on. "That was a genius move! I don't know what I would have done without you. We're leaving tonight," he rushed on. "All of us." Dora looked away.

"How?" she asked, her eyes on the Caves at the bottom of the hill.

"Everyone's meeting in the pool shed. We'll escape from there," Spencer explained quickly. "I'm going to get Darwin now—"

"Take me to B.D. first," she interrupted. "Then bring Darwin to us there."

"But it's faster if—" Spencer started to protest.

"Please do what I'm asking," Dora's eyes locked on Spencer. He hesitated. "It's time I spoke to my brother."

Spencer looked down at the Caves. "You won't hurt him?" Dora had proven Spencer could trust her, but could B.D.?

"I promise." Dora's voice was solemn.

"All right, then we'd better hurry." Spencer pulled his night-vision goggles back down over his eyes. He turned and ran out of Dora's home, careening down the hill as fast as he could to the Caves. Dora stayed right beside him the whole way.

When they reached the door to B.D.'s cave, Spencer dropped his bag to the ground and started searching for his lock-picking kit. Just as he pulled it from his mission pack, a ring with eight keys on it dangled in his face. Dora was holding it in her mouth.

"Thank goodness." Spencer cast the lock-picking kit aside and started trying the keys. B.D. watched through the glass window. When Spencer fit the right key into the lock, he paused. He could hear B.D. grunting, probably urging him to open the door.

"You promise you won't hurt B.D.?" Spencer repeated. Dora's eyes were locked on her brother. She didn't even glance in Spencer's direction when she answered.

"Yes."

Spencer swung open the door and let Dora step through. He grabbed his lock-picking kit and used it as a doorjamb, propping the door to B.D.'s cave open. At least if Dora lost her temper, B.D. would have some chance to escape.

Spencer glanced into B.D.'s cave as he put his mission pack on. B.D. was saying something in Ragayo Spencer couldn't understand. Dora looked calm.

"Disconnect," Spencer whispered, then turned and left

the Caves. He ran back up the hill to Pam's house, his legs burning with every step. "B.D.," he said, trying to connect his Ear-COM to the one he'd dropped into the tank for Mom, Dad, and Uncle Mark.

"Spence," Uncle Mark replied. "We're out. About to arrive at the pool shed."

The news that Mom, Dad, and Uncle Mark had escaped from the Aqua Theater gave Spencer a sudden burst of energy. He charged through Pam's front door and headed for the stairs.

"Have you seen Aldo?" he asked.

"We heard the guards chasing him a few minutes ago. Did you talk to Evarita?"

"Yes," Spencer answered, stepping onto Pam's second floor. "She'll be ready." He was breathing hard, and his side was cramping. Spencer walked into Pam's office and leaned against the desk, trying to catch his breath. "I have to get the cub, Uncle Mark. I'll see you in the shed."

"All right, Spence. Disconnect."

When Spencer had finally caught his breath, he pushed himself away from Pam's desk. Before he could step toward Darwin's room, a flash of movement on Pam's computer screen caught his eye. He leaned closer to the computer. Its screen was filled with a surveillance feed.

"This explains how he knew about the escape," Spencer whispered. The video on Pam's screen was of the Aqua Theater. Pam had his own personal security camera trained on the area where he was keeping his captives. There was another flash of movement on the screen, and a guard raced in front of the glass building. The first movement must have been Aldo. *They haven't caught him yet!* Spencer thought, heading for Darwin's door. He switched on the light and immediately set to work making a rope sling for the cub.

"Anbranda," he growled softly as his fingers knotted and wound the rope over his shoulder. A second later, Darwin's fuzzy head poked out of the cave. He blinked sleepily at Spencer as he trotted over, sniffing curiously the whole way. He snuffled against Spencer's hand where blood was drying from the slice Pam had given him. "Just a scratch," Spencer said, tying the last knot in the sling. "Ready to go meet your uncle?" Spencer reached forward and picked up Darwin. The cub wriggled around and flailed his paws, but after a few tries, Spencer had Darwin securely tucked into the rope sling at his chest.

"All right, let's just tell your mom we're on the way," Spencer whispered as he stood up and headed for the door.

"Aldo," he said, connecting his Ear-COM to the one Dora was borrowing.

"You don't understand," Dora was saying. "You couldn't possibly understand what it has been like."

Uh-oh. Spencer picked up his pace. It didn't sound like things between Dora and B.D. were going too well.

37

By the time Spencer arrived back at B.D.'s cave with Darwin securely strapped to his chest, things between Dora and B.D. seemed to have improved. The two bears were facing each other, Dora on all fours and B.D. sitting back on his haunches. Spencer had listened over the Ear-COM to Dora's side of the conversation for only as long as it took to get from Pam's house to the Caves, but in that time, the anger had faded from Dora's voice. It sounded as though she was finally accepting that B.D. had never meant to abandon her.

Spencer paused outside the door, afraid to interrupt the bears, but they didn't have time for a long reunion now. They had to leave Hidden Rock Zoo before Pam got free and found a way to stop them. Spencer pushed open the door. Just as he entered the cave, he heard B.D. growl.

"*Yi hu aro valu,*" he said.

"*With you I am home,*" Dora's growls to B.D. translated through Spencer's Ear-COM.

A moment passed in silence. Then B.D. and Dora seemed to notice Spencer at once. B.D.'s eyes snapped to Darwin, who started to bawl for Dora. B.D. said something in Ragayo that Spencer couldn't understand.

"My cub," Dora replied. "Darwin."

"We should go," Spencer said urgently. He motioned to B.D. that they needed to leave quickly. The bear tried to conceal a wince as he moved to all fours, approaching Darwin.

"I want you to take him to Bearhaven with you," Dora announced. B.D. turned back to his sister, then started to grunt and growl a steady stream of Ragayo.

"You're coming with us," Spencer said once B.D. had finished.

"No." Dora's eyes were on B.D. "Pam is planning his attack on Bearhaven. I want to help you stop him, but I can be more help to you if I stay here. He trusts me and keeps me close to him; I can learn information that could help you protect yourselves. I can weaken him and his plans if I'm here—"

B.D. interrupted her, urgent Ragayo pouring out of him.

"B.D., what's the point of my leaving now to live in Bearhaven, if I only have a few weeks of freedom before Pam destroys it and captures us all? I'm not leaving with you tonight. But I need you to take Darwin."

Spencer wrapped his arms around Darwin, clutching the cub closer to him. How could they separate Dora and her son? Darwin needed his mother. "He should be with you," he said. Darwin's cries got louder, and Spencer couldn't help but think the cub understood the conversation and was protesting now, too.

"He will be, when I'm free from Pam, when we're all safe in Bearhaven. I have lived in captivity for almost fifteen years," Dora said. "We were only a little older than Darwin is now when we were captured at Gutler, B.D. I don't want the same life for Darwin. Pam has humans raising him here. I want my cub with bears. With you, B.D. You can keep him safe. I can't. Not while I belong to Pam."

Spencer looked back and forth across the three bears. B.D. growled something.

"He's worried Pam will know I've already helped you," Dora translated for Spencer.

Spencer looked at B.D., the bear's face was pained. He had to look away. It must have been settled between the bears already, Darwin would leave Hidden Rock Zoo tonight, but Dora would stay behind.

"We can leave you tied up in here," he said quietly. "He won't suspect you then."

"Spencer will tie my paws and close me in here when you leave," Dora repeated Spencer's plan. B.D. nodded solemnly. He stepped forward and lifted Darwin out of the sling at Spencer's chest, grabbing the cub gently by the scruff of the neck. He set Darwin down on all fours, and the cub scrambled over to Dora immediately.

Spencer pulled the rope off himself as quickly as he could. Dora lay down, then rolled onto her side, extending her legs. Darwin pounced on her, playing.

"Disconnect," Spencer whispered, crouching down beside Dora. He didn't think he could bear to hear what Dora would say to Darwin now, before parting with him for who knows how long. Spencer stayed focused on Dora's paws and the knots he was tying in the rope so it would look as if Bearhaven's team had captured her and left her in B.D.'s cave in his place. When Spencer was done, he stood up and looked at B.D. The bear was watching Dora and Darwin together. Even with her legs bound, Dora was affectionate with her cub.

We're running out of time, Spencer thought. He reconnected with Dora's borrowed Ear-COM. "It's time for us to go," he said.

"All right, good luck," Dora answered. "Hopefully"— she paused as Darwin poked his snout right up against hers—"it won't be long until we're all together again," she finished.

"Thanks for all your help, Dora," Spencer said, unsure of what else there was to say. He leaned down and took the Ear-COM out of her ear, slipping it back into his pocket as he stepped away to give B.D. room to say good-bye.

B.D. stepped forward a little unsteadily. He headbutted Dora gently, growling, then picked Darwin up in his mouth and turned to Spencer, passing him the cub. Spencer took Darwin in his arms. The cub tried to wriggle free. A lump rose in Spencer's throat. He turned and headed for the door. B.D. padded along beside him.

Darwin cried out for Dora loudly when they stepped out of the cave and Spencer started to panic. If they couldn't calm the cub down Darwin would give them away immediately. B.D. started to growl softly, and after a moment, Darwin was quiet.

Spencer led the way into the alley behind the Caves, then broke into a jog, watching carefully to see if B.D. could keep up. The bear limped but stayed right beside Spencer as they crossed the short, dark distance between the Caves and the Seaport Pools.

38

Spencer pushed open the door to the pool shed and someone immediately grabbed him.

"Ahh!" he gasped, struggling to keep hold of Darwin as arms wrapped around him. Just as he was about to panic and tell B.D. to run for it, a scruffy beard scratched his forehead and bandaged hands gripped him by the arms.

Dad wrapped Spencer up in a tight hug as Darwin scrambled out of Spencer's arms and jumped to the floor. "You're okay," Dad said.

"I'm fine," Spencer answered, hardly believing he and Dad were finally together. Over Dad's shoulder, he saw Mom, looking on. She crouched to scoop up Darwin who was running around the shed, tripping over his own paws. Once she had a firm grip on the cub, she stood up and rushed over to Spencer. Dad stepped aside, and Spencer was wrapped up in another tight hug.

"Where's Aldo?" Spencer asked, forcing himself to stay focused.

"He hasn't gotten here yet," Uncle Mark said.

Hasn't gotten here yet? Aldo should have been able to outrun the guards by now. Where was he?

"Where's Dora?" Mom asked.

B.D. grunted beside Spencer. Dad was shining a flashlight on the bear's wounds. Spencer reached into his pocket and retrieved Aldo's Ear-COM. He handed it to Dad.

Dad said something to B.D. in Ragayo, then fit the Ear-COM into the bear's ear.

"Team," Spencer said once the device was in, "Dora's not coming."

Mom protested, but Spencer couldn't hear her. Evarita's voice was suddenly in his ear.

"Team, are you ready?" she said. "I'm on the way. Coming for you now."

"We don't have Aldo," Spencer answered. His heart started to beat faster. "We can't leave without him." Spencer saw Mom and Dad exchange a look, and for the first time, he realized his parents had geared up for the escape. Uncle Mark had, too. They each had a coil of rope crossing their chest, and a flashlight, and tools poked out of their pockets. They must have searched the shed for anything they might use. They were operatives after all.

"How long can we wait, Evarita?" Uncle Mark cut in.

Please say we can wait . . . But Evarita didn't say anything.

"Evarita," B.D. barked. "How long do we have?"

"She's gone." Uncle Mark lifted a hand to his ear as though adjusting the translating device. "We've lost our connection with her."

"What does that mean?" Spencer looked to his parents.

"It means the signal blocker is back on," Mom answered. "Pam and his guards are regaining control of the property."

"We have to move now," Uncle Mark said, taking charge.

"Evarita's on the way," he updated Mom and Dad on the plan. "We have to get to the front gates while Pam and his guards are still trying to get things under control."

"What about Aldo?!"

Before anyone could answer, Pam's voice filled the pool shed, blaring out of a speaker beside the door:

"Now. I'm. Angry."

Spencer balled his hands into fists, trying not show how scared he was. Suddenly, blinding light poured in through the shed's windows. He ran to the closest one. Outside, it was as bright as day. Spotlights were blasting down on Hidden Rock Zoo. The wall surrounding the property was topped by huge lights. He backed away from the window, dropping his night-vision goggles to the floor. Mom reached out and grabbed his arm, pulling him toward her. Darwin gave a frightened cry.

"Every door and window on this property is alarmed," Pam practically shouted through the intercom. "The minute you move, my guards will find you. And I *promise* they will NOT be friendly."

Spencer gulped. He didn't know how they were going to get out of here, but Uncle Mark was right, they had to move now.

"I can only hope your beloved bears in Bearhaven are this easy to defeat," Pam went on. "And by the way. The front gates. Are. Closed." The speaker went silent.

"What did he say?" B.D. asked urgently.

"The front gates are closed. When we open a door or window, the alarm will go off, and they'll know where to find us. He's mad," Uncle Mark quickly updated the bear. "We have to make a move now. If they're waiting for an alarm to go off to locate us, the guards will be sent here as soon as we open the door. They'll expect us to head straight for the front gates."

"But we'll loop through the garden and head for the gates from the opposite side," Mom cut in. "We'll search for Aldo on the way."

"Right," Uncle Mark agreed. "B.D., can you run? We have to take the long way to the front gates."

"I can run," B.D. answered.

Spencer slipped his mission pack off his back. He unzipped it and turned it upside down. Emptying the contents onto the floor. He grabbed his hammer, his slingshot and his flashlight and shoved them into his pockets. He'd have to do without the rest of the supplies.

"Spencer, what are you doing?" Dad asked.

"I need to be able to carry Darwin." Spencer put the backpack back on. "Mom, can you put him in the bag?"

"Good thinking, Spencer," Mom said, settling Darwin in the backpack. The cub sniffled at the back of Spencer's neck and nipped at Spencer's ear.

"He's in." Mom zipped the bag up to hold Darwin's body inside.

"What happens when we reach the front gates?" Spencer asked.

"We fight our way through," Uncle Mark said solemnly.

"How?" Spencer looked around the room. Everyone's expressions were grim.

Dad spoke up. "However we have to."

39

"Everyone ready?" Uncle Mark asked, looking back over his shoulder. Behind Uncle Mark, Mom and B.D. stood side by side, and behind them, Spencer, with Darwin on his back, stood next to Dad. They were going to stick together, all of them running from the pool shed to the opposite side of Hidden Rock Zoo, then to the front gates from there. Uncle Mark would take the lead. Mom was to stay with B.D. If his pain got too bad to keep running, Mom would stay with him and alert the others that they needed to find a way to move him. Spencer was in charge of getting Darwin to safety, and Dad would be last, watching for guards who might pursue Bearhaven's team from behind.

"Ready," Spencer said. His answer was quickly followed by *ready*s from everyone else. Dad reached over and squeezed Spencer's shoulder reassuringly with one bandaged hand. Just then, Uncle Mark pushed open the pool shed door. An alarm screeched on, red lights flashed throughout the shed, and Uncle Mark broke into a sprint.

Mom and B.D. followed Uncle Mark. B.D. stumbled when he lunged forward but regained his balance and took off after Uncle Mark at a pace Spencer wasn't even sure he could match. But now was the time to try. Spencer and Dad burst out of the pool shed, into the bright lights blasting down on Hidden Rock Zoo. Darwin started to hum, scared.

Behind him, Spencer heard Pam's voice yelling through the intercom. "We have you now!"

"That's what you think," Spencer muttered picking up his pace. As he ran, Spencer stayed close to B.D. and Mom, but he searched the zoo around him for Aldo. Where was his teammate?

As they were approaching the garden, Spencer saw Uncle Mark disappear through a break in the trees surrounding it. Mom and B.D. weren't far behind.

"Hey! Stop where you are!"

"This way!"

"They're heading for the garden!"

"Stop right there!

The sounds of guards yelling and running hit Spencer. He tried to turn, to see how close the guards were.

"Keep running!" Dad shouted. Spencer hurtled through the break in the trees and onto the white stone path that wound throughout the garden. His legs were starting to burn, but he couldn't stop now. He could feel Dad right behind him, and Darwin bouncing against his back. They were halfway across the garden when Spencer heard Uncle Mark yell.

"Head for the fountain," he ordered. Spencer craned his neck to see what was going on up ahead. Two uniformed guards were barreling through an opening in the trees on the far side of the garden. Spencer looked over his shoulder. Guards were rushing in from that direction, too. He turned, ready to race down the steps curving around Pam's giant bear fountain, but a huge guard was there, running straight at him.

"Stay where you are, kid!" the guard yelled.

Spencer panicked, he took a step back.

"Jane!" he heard Dad yell. A rope flew in front of Spencer, and an instant later, the guard fell, smashing face-first into the stone steps. Mom and Dad were crouched on either side of the steps, holding a rope taut.

"Nice!" Spencer cheered, seriously impressed.

"There are more coming!" Mom yelled. Uncle Mark turned back.

"We're surrounded!" Spencer screamed.

"Not yet!" Uncle Mark pointed to the marble courtyard at the middle of the garden. If they ran straight across it, they may still be able to get away. Spencer sprinted straight for it. But a moment later, the deafening sound of a helicopter and a sudden strong wind stopped him in his tracks.

"Get down!" Dad shouted. Spencer crouched to the ground. Dad was on one side of him, and Mom was on the other. They wrapped their arms around Spencer and Darwin. Spencer looked up. The helicopter was hovering over Hidden Rock Zoo! It was getting lower and lower.

"It's landing on the courtyard!" he shouted over the sound.

"Do you think it's—" Dad started to yell back, but a voice in Spencer's Ear-COM drowned him out.

"All right, team," Evarita said. "Let's get you out of here." The helicopter set down on the marble courtyard.

40

The noise of the helicopter was deafening, and the wind it created in Pam's garden threatened to throw Spencer off his feet. He ran straight at the helicopter anyway. Uncle Mark reached the helicopter first. A big door in the side was open. Uncle Mark leaped into it, then turned to help B.D. in.

Mom reached the helicopter next. She climbed in, then turned back. Spencer could tell she was yelling his name, but he couldn't hear her. He was a few paces away from the helicopter when suddenly the waterfall stopped flowing, just like it had on the night of Pam's auction. This time, though, when the waterfall stopped, it didn't reveal Pam at the bottom of the slick black marble slab. It revealed a bear.

"Aldo!" Spencer screamed. His voice was drowned out by the helicopter. Spencer ran faster. When he reached the helicopter, he slipped the backpack off and handed it to Mom, who was leaning out, reaching for him. She grabbed Darwin, then called for Spencer to get in. "Aldo's over there!" he yelled back, pointing to Aldo's slumped body.

Spencer raced toward the bridge. As he ran, he realized his sneakers were splashing through water. The moat around

the marble courtyard was rising. Pam must have sent the water from the waterfall into the moat! If it got too high too quickly the helicopter would get trapped here!

"Spencer!" Dad yelled right behind him. Spencer didn't turn back. He wasn't leaving without Aldo. Even if that meant he wasn't leaving tonight. When he reached the bear, he knelt beside him.

"Aldo!" he yelled. Aldo blinked groggily at Spencer.

Dad fell to his knees beside them. "He's tranquilized!"

"We have to get him to the helicopter!" Spencer looked over his shoulder. Uncle Mark was running toward them.

"We have to get out of here!" Evarita yelled over the Ear-COMs. "The water's getting too high! I don't have more than a minute!"

"We're coming!" Spencer got to his feet and hooked an arm under one of Aldo's legs, trying to pull the bear. Dad took the other side, and then Uncle Mark was beside them, grabbing hold of the bear.

"Come on, Aldo!" Spencer screamed as he, Uncle Mark, and Dad dragged Aldo forward. They pushed and pulled him as fast as they could. The water on the marble made it easier. Aldo's body skimmed across it, and in just a few seconds, they were at the door to the helicopter. But the guards were almost there, too. Four of them had already crossed the rising moat and were wading through the water, shouting.

"Ten seconds!" Evarita yelled.

B.D. reached his head down and grabbed Aldo by the scruff of the neck. Dad and Uncle Mark pushed from the ground, hoisting Aldo into the helicopter.

"STOP WHERE YOU ARE!" someone shouted.

Spencer spun around. One of the guards was racing straight at him. A scream got choked in Spencer's throat. He wished he could reach for his jade bear now for strength, and bravery—

Then Spencer remembered the stone bear in his pocket. He grabbed it and in one smooth motion pulled it out of his pocket, wound up, and chucked it hard at the approaching guard. It hit the guard square in the nose. He let out a yell and stopped where he was. Spencer turned back to the helicopter.

Mom leaned out of the open door and grabbed Spencer's arm, pulling him into the helicopter. Dad and Uncle Mark turned, fighting two more guards. The guard attacking Uncle Mark fell to the ground. Uncle Mark turned and joined Dad in his fight.

"I'm leaving. Now!" Evarita yelled.

"Dad!" Spencer screamed. They were starting to lift from the marble courtyard.

"Now!" Dad yelled. At the same time, both Dad and Uncle Mark turned and launched themselves into the rising helicopter. The guard beside them reached for Uncle Mark's leg through the open door, but Mom kicked his hand away.

Evarita propelled the helicopter straight up. As they rose, Spencer caught sight of Pam. He was standing on the top of the waterless waterfall. A guard was on one side of him. Dora was on the other. Pam's arms were crossed. His long claws curved into view, and his face was stony as he glared furiously at the helicopter. Dora rose onto her hind legs. Spencer guessed she was huffing and baring her teeth. She raised a clawed paw, striking out into the air toward Bearhaven's escaping team.

Spencer smiled. To Pam, Dora's gesture would look like a threat, but Spencer knew she was really giving them a victorious wave good-bye.

41

Spencer's hands were still shaking from the mayhem of the escape when he unzipped his mission pack on his lap to check on Dora's frightened cub. Darwin had ducked his head inside the bag and was curled into a little ball. Spencer stroked the bear's ear.

"Don't worry, we're safe now," he whispered, but his words were drowned out by the deafening sound of the helicopter. It was so loud nobody had said a word since lifting off at Hidden Rock Zoo. But Spencer didn't mind that they couldn't talk just yet. For now, having Mom strapped into the seat on one side of him, and Dad strapped in on the other side, was all Spencer really needed. Mom had one hand on Spencer's knee. The familiar gold bracelet she always wore was on her wrist, and the sight of it made Spencer feel safer than he had in weeks.

Dad had an arm around Spencer's shoulders. One bandaged hand hung down beside Spencer's face. Spencer tried to peek at the hand, worried about what might have happened to Dad, but he couldn't see anything. *I don't have to worry anymore,* he told himself. Dad's hands would heal at home.

Uncle Mark was at the front of the helicopter, sitting in the copilot's seat beside Evarita. As though feeling Spencer's eyes on his back, Uncle Mark turned and gave Spencer a wink, then glanced at the bears on the floor of the helicopter.

Spencer followed Uncle Mark's gaze. Aldo was starting to stir. The tranquilizer Pam's guards had shot him with was just beginning to wear off thanks to a second shot Uncle Mark had given the bear just a few minutes ago. Aldo stretched out his legs, his ears twitching. B.D. also watched the younger bear with a look of concern, but of everyone on the helicopter, B.D. was definitely in the worst shape. Spencer could tell the Head of the Guard was putting on a brave face, but the run from the pool shed to the garden, and then pulling Aldo's body onto the helicopter had obviously taken a toll on B.D. Even in the helicopter's dimly lit cabin, Spencer could tell the wounds on B.D.'s shoulder had opened and started to bleed again, and his leg was swollen so big it made Spencer's stomach hurt just to look at it.

After a few more minutes, Evarita landed the helicopter and cut the engine. The deafening noise stopped, and everything was quiet.

"Are you okay, honey?" Mom asked Spencer right away.

"Yeah." Spencer nodded, looking back and forth between Mom and Dad's faces. "I'm great."

Dad chuckled. "Well, that makes two of us." He gave Spencer's shoulder a squeeze and then unstrapped himself from his seat.

"Three," Mom added with a smile.

"Justin just gave me the all clear sign," Evarita called from the pilot's seat, before hopping out of the helicopter through a door in the cockpit.

"All right, let's move." Uncle Mark stood up and rolled open the helicopter's wide side door, revealing Bearhaven's plane a short distance away. There was a man Spencer didn't recognize beside the plane. Spencer could just make him out in the early dawn light. Evarita was walking over to him.

"Who is that?" Spencer asked.

"Justin. He's a friend to Bearhaven, but he works at this airport," Mom explained. "He's helped us on quite a few occasions."

Spencer looked back at the man. He'd heard Uncle Mark and Evarita mention an "airport contact" before. He wondered if Justin was the same one. He'd have to ask Mom and Dad later just how many "friends to Bearhaven" there really were.

"Keep an eye on the bears for a minute, Spence," Uncle Mark said. "We're going to get ready to move them." Uncle Mark, Mom, and Dad left the helicopter through the side door.

"Okay." Spencer looked down at Darwin. His eyes were closed, and his belly rose up and down evenly. The cub had fallen asleep. Quietly, Spencer rezipped the bag. He unstrapped himself and stood, easing the backpack on carefully. B.D.'s eyes were closed. He looked like he was trying to fight off pain.

Aldo's ears twitched again. Spencer knelt beside him and put a hand on Aldo's shoulder. Aldo opened his eyes. He looked around groggily, then slowly growled a few words of Ragayo. Aldo wasn't wearing an Ear-COM. Spencer couldn't understand what the bear was saying, but there would be plenty of time for them to talk later. Right now, all Spencer wanted Aldo to know was that they had done it. They had escaped Hidden Rock Zoo. They were safe.

"Wanmahai," he growled to Aldo, hoping the bear would understand. "We make a pretty good team."

42

Spencer was just settling himself in a seat in Bearhaven's plane when Evarita poked her head into the cabin.

"Spencer!" she cried, rushing over to wrap him up in a quick hug. "Finally! I'm so glad you're okay!"

"Thanks to you I am," Spencer answered. It seemed like Evarita got cooler every time he saw her these days. "How did you know to come in a helicopter?"

"I didn't." Evarita laughed. "We didn't have another truck big enough to fit everyone." She ruffled his hair and headed back toward the cockpit. "I have to get us ready to fly," she called. "But I just had to hug you. I've been worried sick."

"*She's* been worried sick?" Mom remarked walking up from the back of the plane to take a seat beside Spencer. Her arms were loaded with Raymond's fuel bars. "Imagine how I felt when I saw you in the aquarium with all those alarms going off! You, my dear, have had me scared to death since the moment I realized you were going on these rescue missions."

"Sorry," Spencer said sheepishly, remembering the first mission he'd gone on when he and Mom had spotted each other through a conference call between Margo and Pam at Jay Grady's. That was less than a month ago, but now it seemed like another lifetime.

"If I'd only known you would make such an incredible operative." Mom handed him a fuel bar. Spencer puffed up with pride.

"'Incredible operative?' Now that's an understatement," Dad said, joining them. "You know what else is an understatement? That we've missed you like crazy, Spencer." Dad dropped into the seat in front of Spencer and spun around. "We've thought about you every minute of every day we've been gone."

"Me too," Spencer answered. "I don't know what I would have done without Bearhaven."

"Without *Bearhaven*?" Uncle Mark joked from behind Spencer. "What about your dear uncle Mark?"

"That's what I meant!" Spencer laughed, looking over his shoulder. "I don't know what I would have done without Bearhaven *and* my dear Uncle Mark."

Uncle Mark smiled from where he crouched beside Aldo, buckling the sleeping bear in for the flight. Opposite them, B.D. and Darwin were settled together. Dad had already helped them get strapped in, and now Darwin was snuggling up against B.D., who was sitting back on his haunches, gnawing a large knob of ginger root.

"All right, everyone, what do you say we get out of here?" Evarita called back from the cockpit.

Uncle Mark dropped into the seat beside Dad. "I'd say the sooner the better," he called back as he accepted a few Raymond's fuel bars from Mom.

As Evarita steered Bearhaven's plane down the tarmac,

Spencer leaned his head back against his seat. He was suddenly so exhausted that the idea of unwrapping and eating a Raymond's fuel bar was too much for him. He closed his eyes. *Just for a minute,* he told himself.

Spencer woke up on the TUBE with the smell of peanut butter wafting into his nose. He opened his eyes, and for a second, he thought he might be dreaming. Mom and Dad were standing in front of him. Dad was holding a tray of peanut butter toast, and Mom had a pitcher of milk in one hand and a stack of glasses in the other.

"I thought the smell of peanut butter might wake you up," Mom joked.

"You're really here!" Spencer exclaimed. It wasn't a dream! Mom and Dad were really standing right in front of him!

"You bet we're really here." Dad laughed. "Come on, we're almost at Bearhaven, and it's about time you ate something." Dad headed for the door to the dining car.

Spencer leaped out of his seat. "How did I get on the TUBE?" he asked Mom as they followed Dad into the dining car.

"You walked," she answered. "But you were so tired, I think you might as well have been sleepwalking. I'm not surprised you don't remember."

Spencer was happy to see Aldo and Evarita sitting at the table where Dad had just set his tray of peanut butter toast. Evarita had a bowl of macaroni and cheese in front of her, and Aldo looked like he was savoring every bite of his berries and honey.

"You finally woke up!" Aldo exclaimed happily when

he saw Spencer. His BEAR-COM had been returned to his neck.

"I could say the same to you!" Spencer rushed over and gave Aldo a huge hug. "What happened?!" He took a seat next to Mom and reached for a piece of peanut butter toast.

"Well, it was fine at first," Aldo started, licking a smear of honey from his snout. "I was keeping the guards a good distance behind me, leading them all over the zoo property. I didn't want to lose them too quickly, or else they might have gotten back to the guardhouse too soon. But I didn't realize they had a tranquilizer gun . . ." Aldo shook his head. Spencer couldn't believe they hadn't thought Pam's guards might have tranquilizers. He hadn't even known how much danger they were putting Aldo in!

"Since all they did was chase me in the beginning, I figured the longer I ran them around the better," Aldo went on with a shrug. "But I'm guessing they didn't use the tranquilizer gun right away because they hoped to get me over to the Caves and back in an enclosure without Pam finding out. My mistake was running too close to Pam's house. Once I did, they started shooting." Aldo paused to slurp up some berries. "Next thing I knew, you, Mark, and Shane were trying to get me to the helicopter. I could hear you, but I couldn't really get my legs to move. I think I went in and out after that."

Spencer washed down a big bite of peanut butter toast with a gulp of cold milk. "I'm sorry, Aldo," he said. "I didn't even think—"

"Don't worry, little man," Aldo cut him off. "The important thing is we did it! Our plan worked."

"Yeah, the plan *did* work." Spencer smiled. "Where's everybody else?"

"B.D. is in the medical car, and Darwin refuses to be separated from B.D., so Mark is feeding him in there," Evarita explained. "And Marguerite's making sure everything is in order for our arrival in Bearhaven."

Dad pulled an extra chair up to the table and accepted the glass of milk Mom offered him. She set a glass in front of Spencer, too.

"Making sure what's in order?" Spencer asked, wondering what Marguerite, the TUBE attendant, would need to arrange for their arrival. "Like letting everyone know we're coming?"

"No, the opposite," Mom said. "And eat, Spencer, we're arriving soon."

Spencer took a big bite of peanut butter toast and waited for someone to explain.

"Marguerite is making sure the TUBE's arrival in Bearhaven doesn't get announced," Evarita started. "Well, actually, we don't want anyone to know about our arrival at all, except for the bears working in the TUBE station. It's going to be just after dinnertime when we get in. If word gets out that the TUBE has arrived and the team has returned from Jane and Shane's rescue mission, we'll have all of Bearhaven waiting to welcome them. And welcome all of us, too."

"What's wrong with that?" Spencer asked. He couldn't wait to see Kate and tell her all about the mission. What was so bad about her and the rest of Bearhaven being ready to celebrate their return?

"Darwin has been through a lot already," Mom answered.

"We don't want to shock him with an enormous crowd of bears as soon as we get him to his new home.

And B.D. doesn't want all of Bearhaven to know about his condition just yet. This way, he can get some medical attention before anyone sees him."

"B.D.'s going to be okay, though, isn't he?" Aldo asked.

"Yes," Dad said. "B.D.'s going to be okay, but his wounds look pretty bad right now. We'll have a town meeting in the morning once Pinky has had a chance to give him some stitches and bandage him up. And once we've all had a chance to get some rest."

"I guess that makes sense." Spencer finished his first slice of peanut butter toast, and was just reaching for another when the TUBE pulled into the station in Bearhaven. "I thought you said nobody was supposed to be here to greet us?"

A bear was standing alone on the TUBE platform. There was no BEAR-COM around his neck. At first, Spencer didn't recognize him, but then he spotted the furless patch of skin at the bear's jaw.

43

Spencer peeked through the window into the medical car. Aldo was beside him. They'd been told to give the Benally family their privacy, but Spencer and Aldo couldn't resist a closer look.

"I've never seen John Shirley before," Aldo whispered.

"Me neither," Spencer replied. He didn't want to mention seeing John Shirley's photo in Pam's auction. Spencer stared at the bear who had been waiting on the TUBE platform. The furless patch of skin at his jaw had led Spencer to guess his identity. It matched the same marking on B.D.'s and Dora's jaws, the one that Dora had explained came from having to push their snouts through the bars to get food when they were the property of Gutler University.

"How do you think he knew Dora was supposed to be on this train?" Aldo asked. Inside the medical car, John Shirley was playing with Darwin and grunting Ragayo back and forth with B.D., who lay on a bear-sized hospital bed.

"B.D. told me once that when he needs to, he can get a message to John Shirley. B.D. must have told him he'd found Dora." Spencer watched as Darwin climbed up John Shirley's back and playfully nipped at his uncle's ear. "At least he has

Darwin to make him feel better about Dora not being here," Spencer whispered. *And at least Darwin has family to make being separated from his mother again a little less painful . . .* he thought.

"I wonder how long he's been waiting on the platform."

"He got here yesterday," Uncle Mark said. Both Aldo and Spencer jumped, startled, and spun around.

"Uhh . . ." Spencer tried to think of an excuse for why he and Aldo were there.

"We were . . . just checking . . ." Aldo stammered.

"You guys will have a chance to meet John Shirley," Uncle Mark interrupted. "It just probably won't be tonight. Aldo, will you run home and let your parents know we've arrived?" Uncle Mark went on. "I'm sure Bunny would appreciate some warning before the Plains, Evarita, and I all show up in her living room."

"Sure!" Aldo exclaimed, obviously relieved Uncle Mark wasn't mad to have found them looking in on John Shirley.

"Evarita and I are going to go get Pinky for B.D.," Uncle Mark added. "And Spencer, your parents are waiting for you on the platform. I'll see you back at the Weavers'."

"Great!" Spencer and Aldo made their way off the train. Spencer spotted Mom and Dad immediately. They were at the far end of the platform, talking to the bears who had set to cleaning the TUBE.

"I'll see you at home, Spencer," Aldo called. The bear was already stepping onto the elevator up to the clearing inside Bearhaven. Spencer waved as the elevator door slid shut.

"Spencer!" Dad called. "There you are!" Mom and Dad started toward him. Even though Mom's glasses were missing and she looked more exhausted than Spencer had ever seen her, and even with Dad's hands freshly bandaged and his beard grown in, Mom and Dad looked happy.

"It's so good to be back," Mom said when they'd reached Spencer.

"We haven't even made it out of the TUBE station yet," Dad chuckled. He slung an arm around Spencer's shoulders and steered him toward the elevator. Spencer stepped inside first, excited to see all the coolest parts of Bearhaven again with Mom and Dad by his side. The elevator door slid shut, then opened again not a minute later.

Spencer led the way into the clearing inside Bearhaven. It was dusk, and the honeycomb shaped lanterns bordering the clearing were already on. "This is where I snuck out of Bearhaven!" He exclaimed, realizing his parents didn't even know about that. Mom raised an eyebrow at him. "Don't worry, I learned my lesson," Spencer said quickly. "I got me and Kate in big, big trouble that time."

"Sounds like we have a lot of catching up to do," Dad said. He followed the honeycomb shaped lanterns down a dirt path.

"Oh, yeah," Spencer agreed. Suddenly, his mind was overflowing with stories he had to tell Mom and Dad. "I have to tell you about the time Kate and I accidentally took one of Fred Crossburger's water aerobics classes."

Dad laughed. "I've been there."

"And about the time B.D. and I saved Yude from the ocean by Moon Farm," Spencer went on as they started to climb a hill.

"What!" Mom gave him a worried look.

"Don't worry, Jane," Dad said. "He obviously survived."

Mom rolled her eyes.

Spencer was about to list another event he'd need to fill Mom and Dad in on when they reached the top of the hill. They all stopped walking. Bearhaven's valley stretched out beneath them. Little lights were flickering on in the houses and buildings in the middle of the valley. Spencer could just make out the shadows of bears moving around the paths as night fell. He took a deep breath, happier than he'd ever been to be back in Bearhaven, his other home. He looked at Mom and Dad's faces as they surveyed the safe haven they'd built for bears.

Mom sighed, her eyes still on the valley. Spencer could tell she was thinking of Pam, and his horrible plans to attack Bearhaven and capture all its bears. Dad put an arm around her waist and tugged her against his side.

"Hey," he said. "Tonight's for celebrating. You know Bunny Weaver can throw a welcome home party together at the drop of a hat. Tomorrow we'll get back to work."

"Don't worry, Mom," Spencer added. "We're going to stop Pam."

"You bet we are," Mom said, shooting him a smile. "And Dad's right about that welcome home party. Let's get down to the Weavers'."

"Spencer!" Kate was bounding as fast as she could toward them. Spencer smiled.

"Looks like the Weavers are coming to us," Dad remarked.

"What took you so long?!" Kate shouted. "I smelled you an hour ago!"

Spencer laughed and broke away from Mom and Dad, jogging down the hill to greet Kate.

"You did it!" Kate cried when Spencer reached her.

"Aldo and I did!" Spencer cheered, the words suddenly pouring out of him.

"It was crazy! We had to save everyone, Kate!" He wanted to tell Kate everything right away, but she cut him off.

"I found your jade bear!" she exclaimed. "Right after you left!" She ducked her head and grabbed a little pouch hanging around her neck. She jutted her head out toward him, extending the pouch to him in her mouth. Spencer took it, turning it over in his hand. The jade bear slipped out into his palm. "I've been keeping it safe for you." Kate dropped the pouch to hang around her neck again.

Spencer rolled the little stone figurine over in his palm. He was glad to have it back, but it looked smaller than he remembered.

He closed his fingers around the jade bear and slipped it into his pocket. Somehow, he didn't think he'd need to reach for it as often anymore, especially if he had his teammates by his side.

"Thanks, Kate," he said.

"You're welcome," Kate answered shyly, headbutting Spencer. "Now come on, my mom's planning a *party*!"

Property of **SPENCER PLAIN**

Black Bear Cubs!

In the wild, black bear cubs are born in dens in the winter. They weigh 10 times less than human babies and are born blind! Cubs have anywhere from 0 to 4 brothers and sisters in their litter, and they usually stay with their litter mates and mother bear for the first 2 to 3 years of their lives.

The 8 species of bear

- North American Black Bear
- Brown Bear
- Polar Bear
- Asiatic Black Bear
- Andean Bear
- Panda Bear
- Sloth Bear
- Sun Bear

Mission Pack Packing List

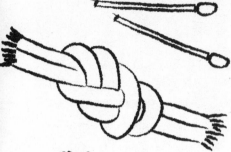

- rope
- Raymond's Fuel Bars
- hammer
- carabiner
- matches
- ginger root
- mirror

- screwdriver
- travel first aid kit
- scissors
- flares
- flashlight
- pocket knife
- super glue

Ragayo Words:

Abragan = for the bears

Wanmahai = teamwork

Yi hu aro valu = with you I am home

Shala = safe

Anbranda = friend

Maruh = hello

Learn more about the bears of Bearhaven, and continue the adventure with Spencer and Kate at www.secretsofbearhaven.scholastic.com.

EGG IN THE HOLE PRODUCTIONS THANKS:

Erin Black, for her continued dedication to the world of Bearhaven, and Nancy Mercado, David Levithan, and Ellie Berger for their support.

Ross Dearsley for capturing the characters of Bearhaven so completely through illustration and Nina Goffi for her beautiful book design.

The marketing and publicity team at Scholastic, for always finding new ways to share Bearhaven with readers: Antonio Gonzalez, Jazan Higgins, Lori Benton, Brooke Shearouse, and Michelle Campbell.

Paul Gagne, Executive Producer, Paul Ruben, Director, and Louisa Gummer, Narrator, for their creative talent in bringing Bearhaven to audio.

For their enthusiastic and ongoing expert advice and contributions to the world of Bearhaven: Dr. Thomas Spady, Bear Biologist, California State University San Marcos, and Dr. Sherri Wells-Jensen, Linguist, Bowling Green State University.

Emma D. Dryden and Elizabeth Grojean, for enthusiastic editorial and managerial creativity and support.

Finally, thank you to all the administrators, teachers, librarians and students who have welcomed Bearhaven into their schools!

ABOUT THE AUTHOR

K. E. Rocha is the author of *Secrets of Bearhaven*, developed in collaboration with Egg in the Hole Productions. She received a BA in English from Trinity College and an MFA from New York University. She has never visited with talking bears, although she often talks to her goofy little hound dog, Reggie, while writing in her studio in Queens, New York.